Dragon Blood 3: Surety

Dragon Blood 3
Surety

Avril Sabine

Cracked Acorn Productions
Australia

Dragon Blood 3: Surety

Published by

Cracked Acorn Productions

PO Box 1365

Gympie, Queensland 4570

Australia

978-1-925131-22-2 (Kindle)

978-1-925617-64-1 (EPUB)

978-1-925131-40-6 (Print)

Genre: Young Adult Urban Fantasy

Copyright 2015 © Avril Sabine

Cover design by Caitlyn Petersen

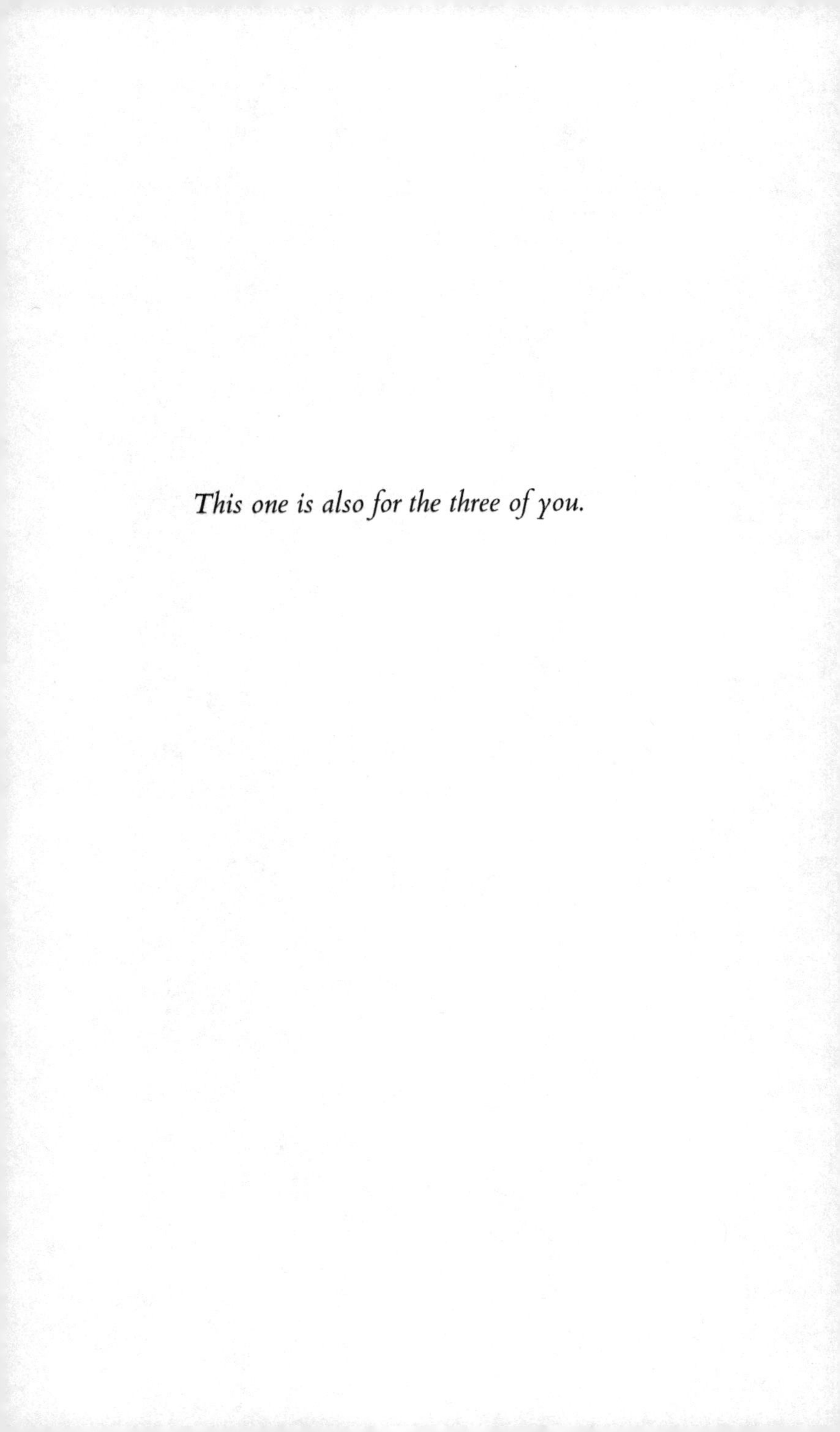

This one is also for the three of you.

Amber learns that her family has a more interesting past than even she could have imagined. That past is now creating problems for her. Negotiations, attacks by an unknown enemy and her mother discovering some of her secrets causes even more complications. The only thing that hasn't changed is that someone wants her dead. She needs to find out who it is before they can succeed and she doesn't get the chance to live long enough to figure out how to solve all her other problems.

*

This story was written by an Australian author using Australian spelling.

Name Pronunciation

Like many names there is more than one way to pronounce the following ones. These are the pronunciations used in this series.

Names:

Alsandair (ahl-san-dare)

Anrai (arn-ree)

Bredon (bread-en)

Chait (single syllable, rhymes with hate)

Daray (dah-ray)

Doneele (donny-lee)

Emlyn (em-lin)

Gair (rhymes with hair)

Gethin (geh-thin)

Isleen (ish-lean)

Kiani (key-ah-knee)

Laren (lah-rin)

Maira (may-rah)

Orin (oh-rin)

Paili (pah-lee)

Queran (qwhere-rin)

Rhobert (row-bert)

Rian (ree-in)

Ronan (row-nen)

Tahmid (tar-mid)

Turi (two-ree)

Other pronunciations:

Erilan (era-len)

Feralenzi (fair-a-len-zee)

Pliethin (plea-thin)

Temolae (tem-oh-lay)

Chapter One

Standing in the hallway, Amber stared at the locked door, her hands clasped together. Behind her she heard Alsandair shift and wished for probably the hundredth time in the past couple of weeks that Rian was with her instead. Rian would never have shown impatience like that.

"Do you want me to open the door or not?"

Amber turned to face Alsandair. His eyes were almost pure gold and he was dressed in black leather pants and a vest. Leather made from the hides of renegade dragons. "You said you didn't even know if you could unlock it."

"I said it was rare that I needed to take such care in opening a door. Normally if I need to enter a locked door, I break it down."

She felt like sighing. Rian never argued with what she wanted, even if it took her ages to figure it out.

Well, rarely ever. "I've already told you I don't want her to know I've been in there." This time the sigh did escape. She had to make up her mind in a hurry. Her grandmother wouldn't be out all afternoon. As it was, she'd waited a fortnight to have the house to herself. Who knew how long before the opportunity would come again. "Okay, but be careful. She can't know we've opened the door."

Alsandair nodded, stepping past her to stand in front of the locked door. He took a small bag of tools from his pocket, that he'd got days ago in preparation for this moment, and began to work on the door. Minutes passed.

Far too many minutes. Amber began to wonder if Alsandair knew what he was doing. Maybe she should have waited for Rian to visit and have him unlock it for her. He'd been really quick at opening the other door. She couldn't help thinking about the medieval armoury that had been behind the door closest to her room. Her grandmother was definitely weird. She was also a bitter old woman who loved to point out people's faults. "Are you sure you know how to do this?"

"Of course I do." There was an edge to Alsandair's voice.

Amber barely held back a smile. She'd momentarily

forgotten how dragons hated to be thought incapable of anything. They were also highly competitive so it was probably a good thing she hadn't mentioned how quickly Rian had unlocked the other door.

There was a click and Alsandair turned to her with a grin. "Got it."

"Yes! Thank you." She threw her arms around him, about to pull away when his arms encircled her, his lips pressing against hers. Shock held her in place for a moment and when she would have pushed him away, it was too late. He was ripped from her arms.

Kade attacked Alsandair, his fist connecting with his jaw. Alsandair threw himself at Kade, attacking with equal ferocity.

"Stop. Both of you stop." Amber jumped out of the way, bumping into the door Alsandair had unlocked, hearing it swing open behind her. Where had Kade come from? She hadn't even noticed him until he'd attacked Alsandair. Had he finally learned how to enter the Void?

They ignored her, continuing their fight. Well, Alsandair had hesitated, but Kade had continued and Alsandair had been forced to defend himself. Amber took another step back, bumping into the half open door behind her as she raised her hands, calling fireballs to fill them.

"If you don't stop I'll throw these at both of you. Do you hear me?" They continued to ignore her. "I mean it." Maybe. She really didn't want to hurt them, but it looked like they weren't going to leave her much choice. Particularly since they looked like they were determined to kill each other.

"Enough!" The word rang up the stairs and Helen reached the top step as the two young men sprang apart to face her. "What's going on here?" Silence met the grey haired woman who wore wire-rimmed glasses and was bony rather than slim. "Well?" Her gaze turned to Amber and her expression went from irritated to furious in seconds. "Get out of there now."

Alsandair's gaze turned to Amber and his face was suddenly filled with horror. "Killer!"

Amber looked from him to Kade, who's expression mirrored Alsandair's when he looked in her direction. "What?" What had she just done to have him call her a killer? The fire in her hands? But that didn't make sense.

"Out! Now!" Helen rushed towards her, a fist raised.

Panicking, Amber extinguished the fire in her hands and, taking another step back, slammed the door shut, locking it before she turned and faced the room. She took a step backwards, colliding with the door. "No." The word was filled with a mix of horror, disbelief and fear. Behind her Helen banged on the door demanding she open it. Amber took a hesitant step forward, reaching out a hand to the skeleton taking up the centre of the nearly empty room. "No." The word was a breath of air as her fingers brushed against the skull. She pulled her hand back, her eyes closing as she took a deep breath, trying to calm herself.

"Do you hear me, Amber? Now!" Helen continued to bang on the door.

Opening her eyes, Amber found that nothing had changed. There was still a dragon skeleton, wired together so it stood in front of her. With a hand pressed against her throat, she took a shaky breath as she tried to figure out what it meant. Why did these things keep happening to her? She ignored the thought that it had been her choice to open the door.

"Amber!"

She couldn't leave Helen bashing on the door all afternoon. Or Kade and Alsandair out there with her. What if she attacked them? Reaching for the door handle, Amber noticed her hand was shaking. She tried to steady it, but had no luck. Unlocking and opening the door, she stood there, staring at Helen who had her hand raised to hit the door again. Amber gestured behind herself. "Explain that."

"I think you already know. Traitor." Helen glared at her.

"Did you know about this?" Kade pointed at the skeleton, his golden brown eyes, that matched the sun streaks in his brown hair, firmly on her.

Amber shook her head. "How could I have? Kade, that kiss-"

"I'm not interested. Once someone tells me what's going on with that," he gestured towards the skeleton, "I'm out of here."

"What do you mean out of here?"

"Who was it? Who changed you?" Helen demanded. "Was it one of them?" She pointed first to Kade and then to Alsandair.

Amber ignored Helen, her gaze still on Kade. "What do you mean out of here?"

"We're over."

"No!"

"You seriously didn't think I'd accept that." This time Kade gestured towards Alsandair, who'd moved closer to Amber.

"Nothing happened. Not really. I was just about to push him away. And where did you come from anyway?"

"Nothing happened? Are you trying to tell me you didn't kiss him?"

Amber shook her head, ignoring Helen's demands to know what was going on. Convincing Kade was more important than paying attention to her grandmother. "Of course I didn't. He kissed me."

"I will believe you, on one condition."

Amber frowned, not making any sense of Kade's words. "What do you mean? There shouldn't be any conditions. You should just trust me."

Kade laughed, a sharp sound. "Do you know nothing about us after all this time?"

"Death," Alsandair said.

Kade nodded and Helen fell silent.

Amber's mouth dropped open and she tried to speak. Death? Alsandair's? For a kiss? "You've got to be kidding."

"Not at all."

"I–" Amber broke off. Why did her life have to constantly go out of control like this? How could she agree to that?

"That's what I thought." Kade vanished.

"Kade! No!" Amber took a step forward. He was gone. Standing in the place he had been felt no different. He could obviously use the Void now.

"Him! He's the dragon?" Helen demanded.

Shaking her head, Amber looked from Helen to Alsandair, not knowing what to do or say. She had to go after Kade. There was no way she was going to lose him over a misunderstanding.

"He knows, doesn't he? He knows I can't tell anyone or do anything. Is that what this is all about? Are they testing me? Forty years ago I turned my back on my family and friends for Charles and Roger. Why would I risk them now?"

Amber tried to make sense of her grandmother's comment. She knew Charles was her grandfather's name. A man who'd died long before she'd been born. "Who's Roger?"

"My son. He was six-years-old when they took him. Only a little boy. No threat to anyone."

"Mum? What's going on?"

Amber stepped forward to look down the stairs at her mother. From the look on her face, learning she had a brother was as much of a shock as learning about an uncle had been for Amber. What had made her think opening the second locked door was a good idea? Now the afternoon was turning into a complete disaster.

"What are you doing here, Donna?" Helen demanded.

"I live here. Who's Roger?"

"Don't be smart with me. I'm the one who let you live here. What are you doing home now? You're meant to be out with that man you're dating. The one you're too ashamed to bring home," Helen said.

"A patient called him. Who is Roger?" Donna started up the steps.

Amber felt Alsandair step closer to her and she wanted to push him away. What had he been thinking?

"I don't know why you're dating a shrink. As if we need anyone around here wanting to mess with our heads." Helen moved away from the stairs, heading for the unlocked door.

"Oh no you don't." Amber hurried into the room.

"Get out of there now." Helen glared at her.

"Amber! What do you think you're doing in-" Donna broke off as she stopped in front of the room, her eyes opening wide.

Alsandair slipped past the two women in the doorway to stand at Amber's shoulder. *"How do you want to deal with this?"* He asked Amber.

Amber shot a dark look at Alsandair. "I don't need any more help from you today."

"Not even my death?"

Chapter Two

Amber dropped her gaze to the polished timber floorboards. "I should have known it was too good to last. Fourteen days of nothing out of the ordinary happening. No attacks being planned, no assassins hiding around every corner, no Ronan and not a single nightmare. I should have known."

"Assassins?" Donna almost squeaked the word.

Helen turned on her daughter. "Will you stop being so weak all the time? Show some backbone. And don't water up like that. Tears are for the weak."

"If you wanted my death you shouldn't have stopped the fight," Alsandair said. "I won't go meekly. If he wants my death, he'll have to earn it."

"No one's going to die," Amber snapped. "All that's going to happen today is someone telling me why there's a dragon skeleton in this room and an armoury in the other one."

"You've been in there too?" Helen demanded. "You've got to pry. You can't leave anything alone. I took the pair of you in and this is how you repay me. Traitor!"

"Stop calling me that." Amber yelled the words, battling the panther that wanted to break free. She couldn't turn into a wild animal with her mother and grandmother staring at her. There was a very good chance she'd probably attack her grandmother if she did. "Who murdered this dragon?"

"Murder! And you say you're not a traitor. Only a traitor would think it murder. Who made you? Tell me." Helen stepped closer, sending a glare to Alsandair when he stepped between her and Amber. "Get out of the way, boy."

Amber waved him back. "I'm not a traitor."

Donna pressed her hands to her mouth. "I remember him. I remember Roger."

Helen sent her a scathing look. "Of course you don't. You were only three. And you cried all the bloody time. Just wouldn't stop."

"He was teaching me to use a cricket bat. He threw the ball to me and it hit my face. My nose bled for ages. But I don't think it was this house."

"We lived in Brisbane before they were taken. You

cried for hours from that nosebleed. You've always been weak."

"Tears don't make you weak," Donna yelled.

"Is that what your shrink's been telling you? What would he know?"

"He's not a shrink. He's a psychiatrist."

Amber raised her hands to grasp the side of her head. Why wouldn't everyone stop fighting? "Enough!" The bedroom light bulb shattered, raining glass on her.

Donna pointed at her daughter. "Your hands are on fire." She sounded hysterical.

Amber extinguished the flames before dusting the glass from her head and shoulders. "The dragon skeleton." Her words were forced out from between clenched teeth. Why couldn't anyone focus?

"Your grandfather killed it. He wasn't a traitor to the family."

"It's fake, isn't it?" Donna asked her mother before she looked to Amber. "Honey, maybe we should take you to the hospital and have you checked over."

"The only way they'll cure her is by killing her," Helen said.

"Mum!" Donna looked horrified.

Alsandair stepped in front of Amber again.

Amber pushed him out of the way. "She's not

going to kill me. She's my grandmother. Stop acting like you're about to take a bullet for me."

"I wouldn't count on it. If you don't renounce them, you're no longer my granddaughter."

"Oh forget it. I've had enough of all this. I need to see Kade."

"You're not going anywhere. You've got school tomorrow."

Amber shook her head at her mother's words. If she didn't get out of here soon, she'd probably be the one killing someone and her grandmother was currently at the top of her list. "I'll be back later."

"I'm serious Amber. Do you want to be grounded again?" Donna asked.

Amber hesitated, not wanting to be grounded. But it probably would be very bad for her grandmother's health if she stuck around. She turned to Alsandair. *"Can you take me to Kade's house through the Void?"*

"I'm not going to make it easy on him."

Losing patience, Amber snapped. "He's not going to kill you. But if you don't get me out of here right this minute, I might."

Alsandair nodded sharply and stepped forward. Wrapping his arms around her, he took her into the Void.

Amber hated travelling through the Void, but at

least it no longer made her nauseous. It was also the quickest way to get anywhere if you knew how to find the paths through it. And Alsandair did. They arrived out the front of Kade's house, but it was empty. She searched it several times with her mind. It was always possible that Kade was there, hiding in the Void. Except Brann wasn't there either. Mentally searching for Kade, Amber felt a tug from the direction of town.

She sighed. Couldn't he have gone home? Typical. It was going to be one of those days where not one single thing went right. She should have expected it. Life had been too quiet. Of course it was due to all fall apart. She tried not to think about how to deal with her mother and grandmother. Once she'd solved her problems with Kade, then she'd worry about them. The dragon skeleton came to mind. Maybe.

It was dark by the time she found Kade at one of the local parks, drinking with a group of kids from their school. Brann was with him and Jessica was draped all over him, laughing at something he'd said. About to march over there and get rid of her, Amber hissed when Alsandair grabbed her arm, dragging her back.

Kade looked towards Amber, his eyes narrowing as

he continued to stare at her. Brann walked towards her while Kade continued to hold her gaze.

Brann stopped in front of her. "Amber, you need to leave. And take him with you." He nodded towards Alsandair.

Shaking her arm free from Alsandair's grip, Amber continued to stare at Kade. "You better tell him that if he doesn't come over here and talk to me I'm going to make a big scene and draw the kind of attention he really doesn't want." She sent her thoughts to Alsandair. *"Leave."*

"I'll be in the Void if you need me. Call out my name." Before Amber could answer, Alsandair disappeared.

"I'm not waiting all night," Amber warned, her gaze still on Kade.

Kade pushed Jessica away from him, rising to his feet. He strode towards Amber, stopping an arm's length away from her. "Have you come to give me the life of your Gold Dragon?"

"Don't be stupid."

Kade's expression darkened. "You're mine and he tried to take what's mine."

"I don't belong to anyone."

"Then you won't mind if I return to Jessica. She was in the middle of a very interesting proposition."

"No." Amber grabbed hold of his arm when he started to turn away.

"So it's okay for you to kiss someone else, but not me."

"I didn't kiss him. He kissed me."

"I saw you. I was there. You threw yourself at him."

"I was giving him a hug. It was 'thank you' and 'I'm so excited we finally got into the room' and 'I'm so relieved you managed to open the door'. There was never meant to be a kiss. I don't know why he kissed me. I've never said or done anything to make him think that was what I wanted from him."

Kade glanced towards Brann.

"What did he say?" Amber asked.

"Clueless human."

Brann hurriedly spoke. "I didn't say that. Well, not exactly. I said it was a cultural misunderstanding."

"Clueless human, huh?" Some of her anger evaporated leaving exhaustion in its place. "I don't want to fight with you, Kade." She reached out a hand to rest it on his chest.

"Do I get to kill your Gold?"

"Stop being so bloodthirsty."

"It's in my nature."

Amber sighed. "I'll get rid of him."

"You're going to kill him?" Kade looked surprised.

"No. Of course not. I'll fire him or whatever you lot call it when someone's services are no longer needed."

Kade took a step closer. "We'll find you another bodyguard. One who knows you're mine."

"Stop saying that. How would you like it if I went around telling everyone I owned you?"

Kade closed the space between them, a smile forming as he lowered his head, centimetres between their lips. "Tell everyone I'm yours." His lips met hers.

Amber slid her arms around his neck, a willing participant for this kiss. She eventually drew back, her arms still around his neck. "I think my grandma wants to kill you. And I'm pretty sure she no longer wants to marry me off to you. Something to do with turning her back on her family and friends to keep her husband and son safe. She thinks she's being tested and she's not going to fail them."

"Someone holds her family as surety?"

"As what?"

"Hostages for her good behaviour. If she follows the rules set for her, the hostages are safe."

Amber stared at Kade, speechless for a minute. "Someone? A dragon?"

Kade nodded.

"A dragon is holding my uncle and grandfather hostage?"

Kade nodded again.

Surely he didn't really mean that. "For forty years?" It was nearly half a century.

"As long as they need to."

Her family were prisoners of dragons? No wonder her grandmother was so bitter. "We have to find them."

"Amber-"

"No. We have to find them. Would you leave your family locked up somewhere for decades?"

Kade shook his head. "I'll see what I can find out."

Amber opened her mouth to ask him questions about how he planned to find them.

Kade spoke before she could utter a single word. "But in return, you don't argue about staying with me until we find you a new bodyguard."

"I don't have assassins after me anymore."

"No arguing."

She started to argue, then wondered why she was bothering. She certainly didn't want to return to her grandmother's house. How many people kept a skeleton in their spare room? Probably not many. And she really didn't want to stay with someone who'd called her a traitor and threatened to kill her.

"Fine. When can you start trying to find something out?"

"Forty years is a long time to be held as surety. Are you certain you want to find them?"

She hesitated. Her uncle had only been a child. Six-years-old. Had he waited to be rescued? How long until he'd finally accepted that no one was coming for him? "Yeah. I want to find them."

"Okay. I'll see what I can find out as soon as we're home and you've got rid of your Gold. Completely gone, not just hanging out in the Void watching you."

"I'll meet you at your house. I need to talk to Alsandair and tell him-"

"He'll already know. I'll take you home."

Amber slowly shook her head. "I don't know how things are done in your world, but that's just rude in mine. I'll talk to Alsandair, he can drop me at your place and you won't have to see him again."

Kade stared at her a moment before he nodded sharply, striding away from both her and the rest of the people in the park, Brann at his heels.

As soon as the shadows swallowed him, Amber felt him and Brann disappear. She guessed Kade must have taken Brann through the Void with him. "Alsandair." She felt him emerge from the Void, in the shadows not far from her, and moved towards him.

"I've notified Rian and Ronan that you're in need of another warrior."

"Why did you do that?" She felt her annoyance start to turn into anger and forced herself to remain calm. "Never mind. Look, I'm sorry about all this. You lot are very…" Her voice trailed off when all the words that came to mind seemed insulting.

Alsandair grinned fleetingly. "Bloodthirsty?"

"Yeah. Among other things."

"I didn't tell them what happened. It's your decision what you say, but if you could not blame this on me, I'd appreciate it."

Amber recalled Maira once telling her that she was on her last chance as a warrior and wondered if this would cause a similar problem for Alsandair. Although she guessed the fact he was Gold meant there were more opportunities available to him then there were for Maira. Ronan was probably all that Alsandair was worried about. He'd been known to kill people who upset him. "What did you tell them?"

"That you wished a different warrior to guard you."

"I want no warrior to guard me. That's my story. I'm sick of being shadowed by people." Sick of her life being turned upside down. Sick of feeling like she had no control over it.

"Thank you." Alsandair bowed, flashing her another grin. "Are you ready for our last journey together?"

Chapter Three

Amber nodded, not knowing what to say. Words still evaded her when Alsandair left her, with another bow, on Kade's doorstep. She continued to stand there, staring at his door until he opened it.

"Are you coming in?"

"I don't want another warrior. I don't need one." When he looked like he'd argue, Amber spoke the words she knew would help her get her way. "Unless you don't think you're capable of protecting me."

"Of course I can protect you."

It took all her effort to keep a straight face. Dragons were so predictable sometimes. "Then it's settled."

"Not at all," a voice said from behind her.

Amber nearly growled as she turned to face Ronan who'd stepped out of the Void. "What are you doing here? I thought you were busy plotting and planning the capture of your own lands."

"Walk with me," Ronan ordered.

Amber felt Kade step close to her and she leaned back against him. "I'm tired. Can't this wait?" Before Ronan could answer, Amber's phone rang and she drew it from her pocket to stare at the screen. Her mother. Just what she needed. "Yeah?"

"Are you okay? I would have rung earlier, but I've spent all this time trying to deal with your grandmother."

"Yeah." Obviously her mother wasn't happy with her own mother if she was referring to her that way. Amber guessed their argument hadn't been settled.

"How did you disappear like that?"

She didn't have time for an explanation so she said the first thing that came to mind. "Smoke and mirrors." If Ronan's expression was anything to go by, she needed to wrap the conversation up fairly quickly.

"Are you sure you're okay? Look, Amber, I didn't realise your grandmother was having so many problems. I've organised a motel room for us for the night."

"I'm staying at Maira's place."

"I'm not an idiot. I've heard around town that she isn't there now. It's that boy you're staying with.

You're too young to move in with some boy. Do you want me to pick you up?"

Yet something else she didn't have time to discuss. Ignoring her mother's question, she focused on what was important. "What did Grandma tell you?"

"Crazy stuff. Now don't change the subject, Amber."

If she managed to get her grandfather and uncle back, her mother was going to find out crazy stuff was real. If? No, she was going to get them back. "What if I could prove that crazy stuff is real?" She felt Kade tense.

He brushed his lips across her ear. "You can't tell the world."

"Why don't you come to the motel and we'll talk about it," Donna said.

Amber laughed. "There's no need to sound like you're talking to someone who's lost it. I'll see you after school tomorrow and show you something that can prove I'm not crazy."

"Wrap it up, Amber. I don't have all night," Ronan ordered.

"Who else is with you? That didn't sound like Kade or Brann," Donna said.

She hesitated, not wanting to annoy Ronan, but also wanting to find out for certain what her grandmother had said. "What exactly did Grandma tell you? I bet you can sum it up in one word. Come on, Mum. What did she say?"

There was silence before Donna finally answered. "Dragons."

"Yes."

"End the call or I'll end it for you," Ronan warned.

"What do you mean, yes?" Donna asked.

"I have to go. I'll call you back later, Mum."

"I haven't finished talking to you."

"I'll ring you as soon as possible. I have something I have to do first. Just give me a bit of time." Amber continued to watch Ronan who looked thunderous at how long she was taking.

"No. We'll finish this right now."

Amber hesitated again, but this time she knew she couldn't make Ronan wait any longer. "Sorry." She disconnected the call and turned off her phone, slipping it into her pocket. Making her mother angry had to be a lot safer than continuing to annoy Ronan.

"Walk with me." Ronan started to move away, not waiting for an answer.

"Amber–"

She turned to press her fingers against Kade's lips, cutting off his words. *"Please. No more tonight. I'm just–"* she couldn't think of what to tell him, then the word came to her. *"Tired. So tired."* Tired of her life being out of control and having no say over what was happening. Tired of people wanting to kill her and tired of never knowing what to expect.

Kade nodded, reaching up to tuck a chestnut lock behind her ear.

Amber took a step back from him, then another as she continued to meet his golden brown eyes. One more step and then she turned, hurrying after Ronan.

"What's going on, Amber?"

Ronan was the last person she would tell what had happened. He'd probably side with Kade and demand Alsandair's death. Actually, there'd be no probably about it. "I'm sick of tripping over warriors, sick of having no time to myself and sick of everyone trying to run my life. I don't need a warrior to protect me. I can look after myself."

"I will get to the bottom of this. Didn't you say you weren't going to keep secrets from me?"

A plan started to form. "You're really good at finding out secrets, aren't you?"

Ronan shrugged. "Passable."

"Who is better than you at finding out secrets? I need to talk to them."

Ronan laughed. "You can't manipulate me, kitten."

"I'm not trying to. I need to find a," she hesitated,

trying to remember the word Kade had used. "A sure something or other. A hostage."

"Surety."

"Yeah. One of them. Well, actually two of them."

"Tell me."

"Why? You said you're only passable at finding out secrets. I need someone who's a master at it."

"I think I'm going to have to teach you about subtlety. I can see your plan a mile off."

Amber laughed. "Maybe you're so used to everyone having a plan that you're seeing plans where they don't exist."

"Tell me."

"I really don't want to have to explain myself twice. I'll wait until I can find someone who can help me find the answers I need."

"No more games, Amber."

It was his tone rather than his words that convinced her she'd pushed him far enough. "My grandfather and uncle. They were taken forty years ago."

"As surety for who?"

"My grandma."

"Are they still alive?"

Amber nodded.

"You humans are so weak."

"We are not." The words exploded from her and she glared at him.

"To allow yourself to be trapped by another's imprisonment is weak."

Amber opened her mouth to argue, then closed it. She'd be wasting her breath. He didn't see the world the same way she did. "Will you find out where they are for me?"

"What will you do in exchange?"

Why couldn't Ronan do something without expecting something in return? Hadn't she done enough for him? She already owed him a minor favour from when she'd accepted Rian as her warrior. She really didn't want to owe him a second one. "I'll bet you already have an idea in mind."

"I'll think about it. You'll have to give me more information first."

"I don't know much. I'll talk to Grandma tomorrow. If she'll speak to me."

"Why wouldn't she?"

"She caught me with my hands full of fire and called me traitor and wants to know who made me."

Ronan stepped close to her, tilting her chin to meet her gaze. "She's a Knight?"

Amber forced herself to hold his gaze. "I don't know, but I've got a feeling she isn't just a collector of medieval weapons and armour. Not after I found an entire dragon skeleton in the other locked room."

"What!" His fingers tightened on her chin.

"The d–"

"Do you know nothing? For how many centuries will I need to sort out your messes?"

"How the hell am I meant to know anything when no one tells me anything." She pulled away from him.

"Only important members of the Knights are entitled to dragon trophies. To own an entire skeleton means you're probably the leader."

"Grandma runs the Knights?"

"Someone close to her does. Or did."

A sick feeling settled in her stomach. "My family are Knights?"

Ronan nodded. "Dragon killers."

Her legs felt weak and she wanted to sit down before they gave out, but there was nowhere to sit. "I–" Her mind emptied. "But–" Again her thoughts scattered and she shook her head. She had to get a grip. There was no way she could let herself fall apart in front of Ronan. He didn't respect the weak. "We need to find out more information." She couldn't believe this was happening. So much for no more nightmares. She was living them instead.

"Call me when you know more."

Amber nodded, her thoughts still half scattered.

"Go back to Kade and don't return to your grandmother alone. Try and be sensible for once. I won't have you ruin my plans to recapture my lands."

Amber could only nod again. When Ronan continued to stand there, watching her, she realised he was waiting for her to return to the house before he left. She hurried away, aware of him at her back, sensing him disappear into the Void as she reached the front door.

Kade was inside, Brann not far from him. She leaned against the door, unable to face anyone. What was she going to do? She couldn't be descended from dragon killers. Especially not the leader of dragon killers. It was wrong. So very wrong. She felt Kade come closer and forced herself to open the door. The last thing she wanted to do was talk to anyone else. What other bad news would she stumble upon? Anything was possible, especially since she still had to ring her mother back.

When the door finished swinging open, her gaze met Kade's. How was she going to tell him that her ancestors killed his? Reaching for him, she drew him close, putting the task off for a minute.

"Are you okay?"

"I have no idea."

Chapter Four

The next afternoon, after school, Amber cautiously walked towards her grandmother's house, dressed in dragon-leather pants and jacket. The two-storey brick building had to be the ugliest house imaginable and the two balconies looked like they'd been randomly added at the last minute. She stopped at the front door, searching inside with her mind. Only her grandmother was home and she was upstairs in the armoury. She paused, wondering if she should have brought Kade with her instead of convincing him to give her an hour with her grandmother before he collected her.

Telling herself not to be stupid and that it was her grandmother, not an assassin, she entered the house. Closing the door behind herself, she quietly crossed the lounge room, passed through the kitchen and hurried up the stairs, pausing in the doorway to stare at her grandmother.

Helen looked up from the large book she slowly turned the pages of, rising from the small table she was seated at when she saw Amber. "What do you want?" She almost snarled the words.

"Who are you?" Had she ever known the woman who stood in front of her? Really known her?

"So now you're going to start asking stupid questions."

"Oh, I know you're my grandmother." Unless her grandmother was right and she really had brought home the wrong baby from the hospital when she'd had Donna. Amber doubted she'd be that lucky. "What I need to know is who you are in your dragon killing group."

"Knights. We're Knights. Our family have always been amongst the Knight Protectors. Your great-grandfather was a High Protector, as was your grandfather before he was taken."

"High Protector?" Surely that title wasn't as important as it sounded. Her luck couldn't be that bad.

"He was in charge of the entire state of Queensland. Each state has a High Protector and every year they gather and discuss what's on the agenda for the next year. And every five years they meet up in a different international location with foreign High Protectors. Charles was one of the best strategic planners in our country."

Yep. Her luck was that bad. She almost didn't ask her next question, not sure she wanted to know the answer. "Strategic planner?"

"He'd killed more dragons by the time he'd been captured than his father had in nearly a lifetime. Charles would be disgusted to learn a granddaughter of his has become a Dragon Mage. They did it deliberately, didn't they? To punish him for all the dragons he killed."

It was worse than she'd thought. How had this happened? "It wasn't deliberate."

"Don't lie to me." Helen jabbed a finger in her direction. "What are you doing here, anyway?"

"I was thinking I might be able to find out where my grandfather is being held, but-" she couldn't bring herself to say the words she was thinking. She didn't know if she wanted to set a killer free, even one who was related to her.

"This is a trick, isn't it?"

"No. But if he's killed a heap of dragons, I don't think any of them would help me find him."

"Of course he's killed dragons. Look at this." Helen

turned the book around so it faced Amber. "This is full of details about dragons who've killed our people. Ones we've agreed should be killed on sight." She turned the pages. "This one killed your great-great-grandmother. And her, she killed one of your great aunts."

The same sick feeling she'd experienced last night hit her again. She wanted to stop the pages from turning. Wanted to grab the book and flick back until she found the drawing that had looked exactly like Ronan. The dragon who'd killed her great-great-grandmother. What had she done? What would he think when he arrived to find his image on a Knight hit list? He was her only ally she could completely trust. Which, whenever she let herself think about it, terrified her senseless. She fumbled for her phone, dialling his number. His phone rang twice then she heard it in the hallway, Ronan obviously having just stepped out of the Void.

"No. You have to go." Her thoughts were accompanied by urgency as she hung up her phone, hurrying into the hallway. *"Go. Please. It isn't safe here."*

"Who's here?"

Amber searched the area with her mind, finding

only the three of them. *"I'll meet you somewhere else. Just not here. Please go."*

"What's going on out there?" Helen grabbed a sword as she walked towards the doorway.

Amber looked between Helen, who was headed for her, and Ronan who stood in the hallway. *"Go. Please. Before she sees you."*

"You better have a good excuse for chasing me away." Ronan returned to the Void.

Amber put a hand out to grab the door frame as her grandmother pushed past, stepping into the hallway. "Nothing is happening. I thought I saw something, but I must have been imagining things."

"Don't give me that rubbish. There was a dragon out here, wasn't there? I heard a phone ring."

"Mum said she'd meet me here."

"What for?"

Amber nearly laughed as she watched her grandmother flounder as she tried to keep up with the discussion. "What did you tell her to make her think you need to be committed?"

"Things I should have told her decades ago."

"If I can help my grandfather and uncle escape, do you think they'd promise not to attack another dragon ever again?"

Helen laughed. A humourless, mocking laugh.

"Unless he's changed dramatically, I doubt it. Charles would rather die. He wouldn't have been weak enough to give into the demands and let some dragon tell him what he could do if it had been me taken instead of him."

"He'd have let you and his son die?"

"It's our responsibility to prevent dragons from killing humans. It's our sacred duty."

Amber stared at Helen whose eyes seemed to be lit with an unnatural light. She'd always known her grandmother was a bitter old woman, but she hadn't known she was also a vicious murderer. Was her grandfather the same? "Can I look at the book? Maybe take it to my room and read it while I wait for Mum?"

"And have you destroy it?"

"I don't want to destroy it, only look through it. Please, Grandma. I'm trying to learn more about all of this." She took a deep breath, determined to convince her grandmother. She needed to know who else was in that book. Were any of Kade's family and allies? She thought of all the dragons she'd met when she'd stayed at his family's castle. "I only have the dragon's side of things. I want to know your side too."

"You aren't to take it from the house." Helen picked up the book, holding it against her chest.

"I won't."

"This isn't the only one in existence, but I can't go to the other Knights without risking Charles and Roger." Helen held out the book.

Amber took it from her grandmother and slowly retreated to the door, not taking her gaze from her. "I'll bring it back after Mum gets here." And after she'd checked for any familiar faces.

"You better."

With a nod, Amber headed for her room, closing her door and leaning against it. She sensed Ronan's presence the moment he stepped out of the Void.

"What's going on?"

It seemed like that was all anyone wanted to know lately. And she'd love the answer to that question too. "If I show you something will you promise not to break it, harm it, ruin it or in any way damage it?"

"Are you talking about the book you're holding onto like it's a life raft?"

"Come on, Ronan. Your word that while it's in my care today, you can't damage it in any way or cause someone else to damage it."

"Why would I even want to look in that book?"

"Because it has something written about you in it." She held the book behind her back when Ronan crossed the room to stand in front of her. "It's not a long term promise. Just for this afternoon." She knew how little he liked to give promises.

"For this afternoon only. After that I can do what I want with it?"

Amber nodded. "But you can't take it from me, I have to return it to my grandma."

"I accept." Ronan held out a hand.

She reluctantly handed the book to him, open to the page about him.

"What about it? I'm sure I'm in a lot of books on dragons."

"The dragons in here are ones that the book says to kill on sight."

Ronan flicked through some pages. "Paili's in here. They need to update this book. I wonder how many of the dragons in it are dead."

Her fear for him turned to annoyance. "Get yourself killed. See if I care."

Ronan tossed the book onto Amber's bed. "I've been on people's wish lists for centuries. If I worried about every single one, I'd have a miserable existence." He stared at her for a moment. "Surely you weren't worried for me."

"I'll know better in future not to bother wasting my time." He wasn't invincible. And he should know that after being captured by Paili. He'd nearly died.

"What details did you find out that can help me track down the relatives you want found?"

Ignoring his question, she gestured towards the book. She couldn't stop thinking about the information she'd read. "It said you killed my great-great-grandmother."

Ronan shrugged. "It's always a possibility. If a Knight comes after me I'm not about to play nice. Now do you want my help or not?"

She bit back the words she wanted to speak. Wanting to demand if he ever felt remorse. Asking him if he ever regretted a death probably wasn't a good idea either. "I don't know if I should be looking for them. My grandfather is a murderer." She hesitated. "I think my family is filled with murderers." Is that why she'd been able to kill Paili? It was in her blood? No, she couldn't accept that.

"Get names and photos to me. Opening negotiations doesn't mean we have to go ahead with them."

"Why?"

"Be more specific, Amber."

"Why go ahead with this? Maybe my uncle is worth getting back, he was only six when he was taken, but my grandfather…" her voice trailed off and her gaze was drawn to the book on her bed.

"Do I need to rip the rest of that sentence from your mind or are you going to tell me instead of wasting my time?"

Her gaze met his, anger flaring at the thought of him invading her mind. "What if he wants to kill me?"

"You fight and you win."

"Easy for you to say," Amber muttered.

Ronan closed the distance between them. "Do you want to die, kitten?"

She shook her head. Of course she didn't.

"Then fight. It's that simple. Fight and win." He stared at her a moment longer before he spoke again. "Get the information to me tonight. We need to move on this immediately."

"Why?"

"Before someone else realises they have hostages that have gained in importance." Ronan stepped back from her, entering the Void.

Amber swore, wanting to demand that he return. She had more questions and no one to ask them of. Shoulders slumping, she crossed the room to her bed and dropped down beside the book. What was she going to do now?

Not having a clue, Amber picked up the book and leafed through it. She didn't have long to see if there was anyone familiar. Other than Ronan. Her mother would be here soon.

Each page had a drawing or picture on one side and a list of crimes on the back of the page. Only a couple of dragons had an extra page to fit their list of crimes and Ronan was one of them. Most of his crimes were murdering Knights. Why didn't that surprise her? Had they come after him or had he gone after them? And did it matter? He was her ally regardless of what he'd done in the past. The only ally she could completely trust. She couldn't afford to ruin that. Not with how precarious life was amongst dragons.

The sound of the front door opening caught Amber's attention and she tensed, relaxing slightly as she realised it was her mother. There was someone else with her, someone that seemed familiar. She frowned as she tried to figure it out. Then it hit her, he was the man her mother was seeing. The one none of them had met. The shrink.

Chapter Five

Amber rose to her feet, taking the book with her. About time she got to meet him. She reached her bedroom door, but instead of leaving her room, she faced the French doors as she felt Kade step out of the Void and onto her balcony.

Kade opened the doors. "Are you ready to go?"

Amber shook her head.

Kade tilted his head, frowning. "I hear a man downstairs."

"Mum's boyfriend. It looks like I'm finally going to meet him."

"Do you want me to come with you?"

Amber wanted to say yes and drag him downstairs. Instead, she shook her head. "I don't think you should be around my grandma for a bit." Especially since she had an armoury full of weapons.

"It's probably a good thing she can't tell anyone

about me or I'd have failed my test by disappearing in front of her last night."

"Oh." It took her a moment before she could say anything else. "Why did you?"

"I've never been so angry before." Kade entered the room, closing the doors behind him. "You might not like it, but you're mine."

Amber sighed. "We're not going through this again, are we?"

Kade grinned, crossing the room and taking the book from her. He tossed it on the bed. "You can't argue it."

Amber looked towards her bed. "I wish people would stop doing that."

"Amber."

"What?"

"Focus."

She thought back over the conversation. "I am. I'm not a possession."

"Then if you're not mine, I'm not yours and I can take Jessica up on her proposition."

"Fine."

"Fine, what?"

Amber glared at him, not wanting to say the words he expected. Her glare faded and she smiled. "You're mine."

Kade laughed, reaching out to pull her against him. "Yeah, you are too."

"Amber!" Donna's voice came from downstairs.

Kade groaned. "Don't answer her."

"I have to." She reached up, sliding her hands across his shoulders to link them at the back of his neck. "Eventually." She kissed him, ignoring her mother calling out another three times before she drew away from him. "I'll be back soon." She reached for the door.

"What about your book?"

Amber faced the bed, staring at it for a moment. "Look after it for me. I promised Grandma no harm would come to it while it was in my care."

"Okay."

She reached for the door again, hesitating. "Uhm, it's a hit list. I only know two of the dragons in it, but you might know some of them." She hoped that none of the dragons in there were his friends.

"Really?" Kade picked up the book, opening it. "Which ones do you know?"

"Ronan," she muttered. "And Paili."

Kade looked up at her, laughing. "I guess I should have expected Ronan to be in it."

"Just don't trash it no matter what you find."

Kade dropped onto the bed, leaning against the

pillows and drawing his knees up to rest the book against them. "It's okay. I won't damage it. Now go and see your mother and her lover so we can get out of here."

"Oh great, did you have to say that?" She wrinkled her nose. "How am I going to meet him now. That's got to be the worst thought in the world."

Laughing again, and waving her away, Kade said, "Go."

Still shaking her head, Amber slowly headed down the stairs, finding her mother at the base of them. She discarded several comments, making do with giving her mother a hug when she reached the foot of the stairs.

"Are you okay, honey?"

Still holding her mother tightly, Amber nodded. "Yeah." She forced herself to let go.

"Are you sure?" Donna's eyes were filled with worry.

"Yeah."

Donna stared at her for several minutes before she nodded. "I have someone I want you to meet. Come into the lounge room."

Amber followed her mother through the kitchen and paused in the doorway of the lounge room, her way blocked by her grandmother. She couldn't clearly see the man her mother wanted to introduce her to, but his presence seemed familiar. More familiar than it should have for someone she'd only noticed from a distance.

"Out of the way, Mum," Donna said.

Helen didn't move.

"Please Helen, Donna didn't invite me here to-"

Helen interrupted the soothing voice. "I don't know what she told you-"

Amber pushed past both Donna and Helen to stare at the overweight, balding man with faded brown eyes and wire-rimmed glasses. "You!" It was the doctor who'd treated her when she and Ronan had escaped from Paili.

"Rude. No manners, that's what's wrong with you." Helen glared at Amber.

"I didn't know." The man's words were soft, his expression worried.

"You've met my daughter before?" Donna asked.

"Not exactly. I didn't know who she was." He stepped forward, holding out a hand to Amber. "Gary Russ."

Amber ignored his hand. "I thought you were a doctor."

"A psychiatrist."

"There was nothing wrong with my head." She stared defiantly at him.

"Will someone tell me what's going on?" Donna demanded.

"You have to study general medicine for six years to become a psychiatrist."

"How much did he pay you?" Amber demanded, ignoring the argument that started between her mother and grandmother.

"He always pays well for out of hours house calls."

Amber shook her head. "No. To date my mum."

"Nothing. I didn't even know," Gary protested.

At the same time, Donna abruptly stopped arguing with Helen to turn to Amber. "What are you going on about?"

"Bloody interfering dragons." Amber pulled her phone from her pocket.

Helen pointed at Gary. "Don't tell me he's a dragon too."

"Mum! Will you please stop. Dragon's aren't real."

Amber dialled Ronan's number, desperately trying to keep the panther from escaping. She didn't know what would happen if she let it escape, but she doubted it'd be good with how she currently felt. "Stop interfering in my life and leave my mum out of this."

"You were the one who asked me to interfere. I've already told you we can't leave valuable hostages with our enemies. Although I have no idea what that has to do with your mother."

"Gary."

Ronan chuckled. "I know. It surprised me too. I thought she'd have gone for one of the others."

"What? You paid a heap of men to date her."

"Who are you talking to, Amber?" Donna demanded.

"It wasn't like that," Gary protested.

Amber turned her back on them, trying to focus on staying human. "Well?"

"I didn't pay anyone. I organised to meet some of my employees at places I knew your mother would be and then I cancelled on them or told them to entertain themselves because I'd be late. Gary was a long shot."

"Are you sure?" Amber found it hard to believe he was telling her the truth.

Ronan laughed. "Don't get me wrong, kitten. It was deliberate, but I never paid any of them or let them in on my plan."

"What is your plan?"

"Think about it. You have to work this one out for yourself."

Amber growled when Ronan hung up. The sound was far too much like a panther for her liking. She had to get a grip on her anger. Although how she could do that, she had no idea. She faced the other three occupants in the room who all seemed to be talking at once. Rubbing her temples, she considered leaving them to it. "Shut up!"

Donna rounded on her. "Amber!"

She ignored her mother. "This is madness."

Gary chuckled. "I've always thought so."

"How did you get mixed up with Ronan?" Amber still couldn't believe her mother was dating this man. He was nothing like her father.

"I was struggling to put myself through university."

"Who is Ronan?" Donna asked.

"Probably another dragon," Helen muttered.

"Mum! Stop it. No more talk about dragons," Donna said.

Amber took a deep breath, pushing the panther back down. Letting it out might solve some problems, but with the mood she was in, it'd probably cause a lot more than it solved. "Okay, I believe you, Gary. Ronan didn't pay you to date Mum. He was just deliberately, indirectly, responsible."

"Amber, honey, I think it's time we left. Grab some

things. We're staying at the motel until I can find somewhere else to stay for the year. I thought about going back to Brisbane, but you've already shifted schools enough this year."

Amber shook her head, her gaze going from Gary to Helen, completely ignoring her mother's words. "I need names and photos. We're starting negotiations to get our family back." As soon as she had that information she was going. Before she lost control. Hopefully.

"What's the catch?" Helen asked.

Amber was tempted to say there was none, but didn't think her grandmother would believe her. She was also sick of all the lies and shortly she was about to bring a lot of them to an end. "I can't afford to have them used against me. As far as I know, there are only three Dragon Mages and everyone wants us to work for them. Although a few would prefer us dead."

Helen nodded. "Whose side are you on?"

"Mine."

Helen stared at her for a moment, before she nodded slowly. "Maybe you're not a complete loss after all. At least you're not as weak as your mother."

"Mum!" Donna glared at her mother and Gary put an arm around her shoulders.

"I don't need your approval. I never have." Amber

raised her chin, refusing to look away from her grandmother's hard look, barely biting back the words to defend her mother. She didn't need to get into another argument.

"That's good, because you're not about to get it while you're associating with dragons."

"If I hear that word one more time…" Donna let her warning hang in the air.

"Donna," Gary said hesitantly.

"We're going," Donna said firmly. "Get your things, Amber."

Amber finally turned her attention to her mother. "I'm staying with Kade. He can protect me, you can't."

"If there's something wrong we'll go to the police. They'll-"

"No!" Amber, Helen and Gary all spoke at the same time.

Donna looked at each of them. "Will someone please tell me what is going on and don't any of you dare mention the word dragon again or I will call the police."

Amber reached out for Kade. *"Come and keep them safe. I'm going to become a panther and I'm not sure how well I can control it right now."*

"Are you certain this is what you want?"

"I really don't think you should be the one turning."

"That wasn't what I was thinking. What about the goshawk? It might be safer for them."

She could sense him coming closer to her. *"The panther isn't going to take a backseat tonight. Not with how pissed off I am."*

"Then maybe you should leave it for tonight."

"No. Mum's threatening to call the police."

Kade stepped into the room, giving a general nod of greeting.

Helen's eyes narrowed at the sight of him and Gary returned his nod.

Donna pointed at Kade. "Is he the reason you really wanted to see your grandmother today?"

Amber shook her head. "No. I'll see him all night. I don't need to sneak him into my room to see him."

"I've had enough. You can make do with what you've got on you. We're going." Donna reached out, grabbing hold of Amber's wrist.

She pulled away from her mother, taking several steps back. "Kade won't let me hurt you. Everything that's crazy is far too real." Letting the panther escape, she changed in front of everyone, her anger forcing a roar from her.

Chapter Six

Donna screamed and fainted. Gary caught her and Helen screeched, "I knew it. I knew it. Dragon Mage. Traitor!"

Amber's muscles bunched and she prepared to spring at Helen.

Kade stepped in front of her. "Amber. You don't really want to do that. Change back."

Amber snarled, closing the gap between them.

"Amber." Kade crouched in front of her, reaching out a hand, stopping centimetres away.

She tried to push the panther back, but anger kept her from changing. Anger and the instinct to attack those who threatened her. Moving slightly, her gaze arrowed in on Helen. A menacing growl emerged from her.

"I thought it was a dream. A nightmare." Sitting on the floor, Donna leaned against Gary.

Amber turned her head in Donna's direction when she spoke.

Donna struggled to her feet. "We're going back to the city. Immediately."

Amber snarled, growling at Kade when he moved between her and her mother. No one was forcing her anywhere.

Helen laughed, a bitter, mocking sound. "Too late for that. Nothing can fix her but death. Unless someone kills her, she'll well and truly see this century out."

Amber snarled at Helen. She wasn't about to let anyone kill her, especially not her own grandmother.

Kade moved again, trying to draw her attention away from Helen. "Amber. Change. Please. I can't change in front of everyone to stop you attacking them."

She fought against instinct and with one last snarl, changed back, pushing past Kade to face Helen. "How many dragons have you killed?"

"Two."

"What did they do that you killed them?"

"We found them."

"So they did nothing." Her hands curled into fists and she struggled against becoming a panther again.

"They're dragons." Helen sounded like she spoke of a mass murderer.

"Dragons aren't real." Donna's tone was pleading.

Amber continued to stare at Helen. "What about Dragon Mages? Have you killed any of them?"

"There's always a first time for everything."

Amber wanted to wipe Helen's smug expression off her face by telling her that both her grandchildren were Dragon Mages. But it wasn't her secret to tell. "You'd kill your own flesh and blood even though they've done nothing to you." Behind her she heard Gary try and calm her mother.

"I can't believe they're making mages again. I would have thought that after the last time they wouldn't have bothered."

"Last time?" Amber asked.

At the same time, Kade asked Amber, *"What is your grandmother talking about?"*

"When the Knights convinced the mages that they didn't need to be ruled by dragons. The mages took it too far. The Knights had to hunt them down and kill them too."

"When was this?" Amber demanded.

"The witch hunts of the Middle Ages."

Amber couldn't stop looking for some sign that her grandmother didn't mean everything she'd threatened. The hard look in her eyes and the compressed line of her lips made Amber believe she meant every single word. She guessed it wasn't only dragons that were bloodthirsty. "The Knights killed humans." Her words were flat, sounding more like a statement, even though she wanted her grandmother to confirm it.

"You're not human anymore. You're a Dragon Mage. You'll always be a Dragon Mage."

Amber held back the flow of angry words she wanted to spill. Behind her Gary continued to try and calm Donna. Amber barely stopped herself from telling her mother to shut up. When Kade placed a hand at the small of her back, she glanced towards him. He smiled slightly before he returned his attention to Helen. Remembering Ronan's orders, Amber decided she was wasting her time trying to change Helen's mind. It had been made up long ago. Well before she'd even been born. "I need the photos before I go."

Helen nodded, striding towards her bedroom.

Amber stared after her, turning to her mother when she spoke her name. "What?"

"How did this happen?"

She didn't know how to explain. Because her mother had brought her to this town? Because her grandmother didn't have a dishwasher? Because Kade had been distracted? "Random stuff happens. Wrong place at-" she broke off, changing her mind about the words she wanted to speak. "The right time." She smiled when Kade's hand brushed up and down her back several times. Some of her anger faded.

"You can't stay at his home. Not on your own," Donna said. "You're too young to move in with your boyfriend. You're only seventeen."

Amber started to argue that she wasn't too young.

Kade interrupted her, his gaze on Donna. "You're welcome to stay there too."

Amber looked up at him. "Are you sure? And Gary too?"

Kade nodded. *"It's probably safest that she isn't left to wander unprotected while we're trying to get your family back."*

"I don't know if I want them back. My grandfather's a killer. What if he tries to kill you?"

Kade grinned. *"I'll try not to hurt him when I subdue him."*

Amber glared at him. "That's not funny."

"What isn't funny?" Donna looked between each of them.

"Nothing," Amber muttered, ignoring Kade's chuckle. "I need to grab some clothes." She also needed to get the book and return it to her grandmother. When no one argued with her, she hurried from the lounge room, heading for her bedroom.

Staring around her room, she tried to recall the first time she'd seen it. That moment felt like years ago, not months. Her gaze fell on the book, still lying on her bed. Picking it up, she skimmed through some of the crimes, stopping when she reached a dragon that had only one crime listed. 'Suspected of killing Harriet Selton, 1941.'

Amber shook her head when she turned the pages, finding no more crimes for that dragon. Leaving the book open on her bed, she grabbed some clothes, shoved them in a bag and took it, along with the book, back to the lounge room.

"Here." Helen stepped forward, holding out two photos. "They stopped sending photos of Roger with his letters about twenty years ago."

Amber put the photos in her bag. She continued to hold onto the closed book, her finger marking the page. "Is everyone in here to be killed on sight?"

"Yes."

"Even this one." Amber held the book out, open to the page of the dragon with only one crime.

"All of them."

She held Helen's gaze. It never wavered. "What is his crime?"

Helen turned the page. "Exactly what it says here."

"Suspected."

"He's a dragon. Of course he's guilty." Helen's conviction was clear in the tone of her voice.

Amber slammed the book shut, shoving it at her grandmother. "There's no difference between Knights and dragons." Ignoring Helen's arguments, Amber crossed the room to where her mother stood with Gary's arm around her shoulders. "I'll meet you at Kade's."

"How will you get there?" Donna asked.

"It's probably better you don't know."

Helen pointed a finger at Kade. "He's a Gold Dragon. They'll be there in seconds. Once Charles and Roger are safe, he won't be."

Amber was across the room in seconds, her hands curling into fists in an effort not to shake Helen. "You will not harm him. You won't tell anyone he exists." Her voice was low and there were only centimetres between them.

"Don't you dare threaten me."

"Then don't threaten Kade. Getting my grandfather and uncle away from their enemies doesn't mean they'll get to come home. My allies might think it's better they keep an eye on them." And maybe that might be the only way to keep everyone safe.

"Traitor." Helen spat the word out, her gaze sharp.

Kade stepped up behind Amber, wrapping his arms around her, pulling her away from her grandmother. "Time to go."

Amber tilted her head so she could meet his gaze. She hesitated, but she'd had enough. "Yes." She closed her eyes as Kade took her into the Void, opening them when he kissed her. They were at his front door, Brann opening it.

"Prepare Orin and Morgan's old room for Donna and Gary," Kade said.

"Who's Gary?"

"Another one of Ronan's plans," Amber muttered.

When Brann continued to look confused, Kade said, "Donna's lover."

Amber groaned. "Call him her boyfriend. It sounds better."

Brann started to leave the lounge room, speaking over his shoulder. "Updates from Maira are on the kitchen table."

"You go and look at them, I need to ring Ronan."

"Do you want me to stay with you?"

Amber shook her head. "No. I'll be safe."

"But will you be okay?"

Having no reassurance, she shrugged, pulling out her phone and dropping her bag on the floor near the front door. She watched as Kade nodded and walked towards the kitchen before she dialled Ronan's number. "I've got the information you want," she said the moment he answered.

"Good." He disconnected, appearing several minutes later in front of her.

Amber stepped back. "She told me what happened to the last Dragon Mages."

When Amber remained quiet, Ronan finally spoke. "Are you planning to share that information with me?"

She nodded, wishing she could find a way to convince Ronan to protect Kade for her even if she died. If only she had something valuable to bargain with. But she had nothing and the information she'd gained wasn't worth much. It'd be better for her to give it to him. While she took the photos from her bag, Amber told him what she'd learned, finishing with the fact that her mother and Gary were on their way.

"I can't believe she chose him out of all the ones I sent her way. I hope you've got better taste than your mother," Ronan said.

"He's not that bad." Amber felt obligated to defend her mother's choice.

Ronan took the photos, frowning. "This kid looks familiar."

"He's not a kid in that photo. He's twenty-six."

"A kid." Ronan tucked the photos into his vest. "I'll have copies made and return these to you."

Yawning, Amber nodded.

"And get some sleep. You're not still having nightmares are you?"

"No." Although she wouldn't be surprised if she had one tonight after the day she'd had. Her grandmother definitely wanted to kill her. She'd always known she was a bitter old woman, but she hadn't suspected she was a murderer.

"Find other warriors to protect your lands and tell Rian to join you here. At least you let him look after you."

She shook her head. "I don't trust anyone else to protect them."

"About time. I might make a dragon of you yet." Ronan disappeared into the Void before Amber could argue.

"Damn dragon." She stalked to the kitchen where she found Kade sitting, head bent over reports. He looked up to give her a quick smile before he returned to them.

Maybe Ronan was right. Sleep was the best plan. Surely tomorrow had to be better than today. The weekend was always better than a school day.

Chapter Seven

She'd been wrong. Completely and utterly wrong. The day had started fairly ordinary. With breakfast. Then things had gone downhill. Her mother had lectured her, demanded answers and finally ended with, "At least Jasper isn't involved in all this mess."

Amber had barely managed not to blurt out that Jasper was in exactly the same mess, only he'd asked for it.

After Donna's interrogation one of Ronan's warriors arrived to return Amber's photos, only bowing before he left, speaking not a word. She stared at the photos in her hands wondering why the photo of her grandfather was more current than the one of her uncle. Was Roger still alive?

Her uncle, like her mother, had blond hair and blue eyes, but he had a look of mischief in his gaze. The picture had to have been taken in his mid twenties.

She wondered if her mother had ever had that same expression. The photo of her grandfather was of a grim, imposing man with white hair and sharp blue eyes. He looked solid and dangerous. Not someone to be messed with.

Kade walked into the kitchen where she continued to stand, staring at the photos. "Who are they?" He nodded towards the photos she held.

"My family." She gave them to him, the one of her grandfather on top.

Kade stared at the picture. "I'm guessing he's going to be as happy to have me in your life as your grandmother is."

She was pretty sure Kade was correct. "I don't know what to do."

Kade looked up from the photo. "We'll figure it out." He looked down again, shifting the top photo behind the second one. "Who is this?" His voice was sharp.

Amber moved to his side. "My uncle."

Kade stared at her.

Amber waited for him to speak, but he remained silent. "What?"

"I've met him before."

"You have? How?"

Kade gave her the photos. "How long ago was he taken?"

"I already told you. Forty years. And he was six at the time."

Kade tapped the photo she held. "He still looks like that."

"What do you mean?"

Kade turned away to stare out the window. Silence stretched between them.

"Kade." There was a warning note in her voice. He better hurry up and tell her. She was completely and utterly sick of secrets.

He met her gaze. "He's married, Amber. He has three daughters."

"And?" There had to be more. That didn't sound like all that big a deal. People got married all the time. And had kids.

"His oldest daughter is a Gold."

Amber frowned. Gold? "As in a dragon?" Surely she'd misheard.

Kade nodded.

"But he's a prisoner." Why would anyone let a prisoner get married? And obviously to a dragon.

"Not anymore."

"He's not a prisoner." She said the words slowly and clearly, wanting to make certain he understood her.

"No."

Amber stared at him, trying to make sense of everything. "Is his wife a Gold?"

"No. One of her great-great-grandparents were. Or it might have been her great-great-great."

"He's human."

"The base form of his kids is human, but they can change into dragons." Kade grinned. "Were you worried we couldn't have kids?"

She held up a hand, taking a step backwards. "Oh no, don't even think about going there. I've got enough problems to deal with." She mentally searched for her mother, hoping she was far enough away that she hadn't heard that comment. She didn't need any more lectures. Finding her mother outside with Gary, she relaxed a little. "So what's this mean?"

Kade shrugged. "I don't know. But he isn't in a weak position."

"What about my grandfather?"

"I've never seen him before."

Amber tossed the photos onto the kitchen table. "This is great. Just great." Her tone said it was anything but. "I need to ring Jay and tell him all hell's working on breaking loose. Again."

"I need to meet some warriors. I'll leave Brann here to look out for you."

Amber's eyes narrowed. "I don't need a bodyguard."

"They're not for you. They're to replace Maira. When things go crazy, I want warriors I can trust by my side." Kade drew her to him, wrapping his arms around her waist. "Don't leave the house."

"An entire fortnight without dramas. I thought everything was going back to normal. Or as normal as it's possible to be around you dragons."

"Probably the calm before the storm."

Amber opened her mouth to argue, but Kade's kiss stopped her words. When he finally pulled away, she'd forgotten what she was going to say. "Be careful."

Kade laughed. "I'm a dragon. I can take care of myself." He vanished into the Void.

Amber shook her head. If that was true, then dragons would never die. And they did. Far too many of them. She shied away from thoughts of Paili. She needed to ring her brother, not remember old battles. Then she had to start storing more energy. She had a bad feeling she was going to need it. Looking at the six gold bracelets she wore, she made a mental note to ask Ronan where she could buy them. She doubted any human shop would sell bracelets that had been cast with dragon-leather through them. Maybe a dozen more would be enough. She hated to think how bad a situation would be if she needed more stored power than that. The end of the world? She really didn't want to find out.

* * *

Jasper arrived late afternoon. Hearing him drive up, Amber was out the front before she sensed her mother moving. "She's in a really bad mood," Amber said by way of greeting.

Jasper shrugged. "I'll talk her round."

"This might even be beyond you. She's been out the back most of the day. Talking to the shrink. Then she comes inside for a bit, gives me another lecture, throws up her hands, bursts into tears and returns outside with Gary."

"Maybe if you'd compromise about-"

Amber cut him off. "I can't change what I am and neither can you. Compromise is impossible."

"We'll see."

"I won't. She's coming around the side of the house. You go talk to her, I'm fed up with the lectures." Amber strode towards the front door, glancing back once to see her mother throw her arms around Jasper as they met at the corner of the house. Feeling a presence behind her, she whirled, flames in her hands before she had time to realise it was Ronan.

"Much better."

Extinguishing the flames, Amber lowered her hands, not relaxing. "What do you want?"

"Bathroom."

She followed him through the house, turning the bathroom tap on while he closed the door. Making sure other dragons couldn't overhear wasted a lot of water. Maybe she should suggest to Jasper that he organise a running water garden at her house. Her house. The thought just never seemed real. She was too young to own her own house. Pushing uncomfortable thoughts away, she faced Ronan. "What do you need to tell me?"

"We should kill Charles."

"What?" She knew she shouldn't let him, but Ronan always managed to surprise her.

"He's a liability."

"You think everyone's a liability."

"He killed a dragon while he was a prisoner."

Amber stared at Ronan. "Are you sure?"

"Of course I'm sure. They tried to hush it up, makes them look weak, but I found out. Couldn't get all the details, but it wasn't a kid. A male dragon about ninety-years-old. An experienced warrior."

"I don't know what to do." She regretted the words the moment she spoke them. She had to stop acting so weak in front of Ronan.

"Take him out from a distance."

"No! He's my grandfather."

"So? You don't even know him. That man would kill every dragon in existence if he could."

"You want me to kill a man that I'm directly related to."

"I didn't say you had to do it yourself. We'll send an assassin." Ronan paused, watching her carefully. "I could send Doneele's father, Daray."

Amber tried to keep the shock from her face. "How did you know?" Was it impossible to hide any secrets from him?

Ronan laughed. "I guessed. You confirmed."

She glared at him. "Don't you dare harm her."

"She's yours, isn't she?"

"Yes." She didn't even hesitate.

"Then she's safe while you live."

Amber sat on the edge of the claw foot bathtub. "What about my uncle?"

"He's safe. Or as safe as any dragon is."

"He's a dragon?" How was that possible?

"No. Married to one and fathered a Gold. So he might as well be a dragon. It's the old man we need to worry about."

"We're not killing my grandfather."

"Is he yours?"

She stared up at Ronan, trying to figure out what to say. He'd never set a limit, only told her there was one. Now didn't seem like the time to ask him. "He's my grandfather."

"But do you claim him?"

She wanted to be able to say yes, but she couldn't bring herself to speak the word. How many until she ran out of people she could claim? Lowering her gaze to the floor, she said, "I don't know."

"You need to make a decision, kitten." Ronan sat beside her.

"How can I?" She fiddled with her bracelets, checking that all of them glowed with power and she hadn't missed filling any of them. "I don't even know the man."

"Then it should be simple. We kill him."

Amber shook her head. "I can't order the death of an-" she broke off. Innocent man was nowhere near accurate. He was so far from innocent she didn't have a clue what he was. The word murderer came to mind and she pushed it away. "He's my grandfather."

"I once told you this weakness for family would get you killed. Being weak this time might mean the death of others."

Fear hit Amber and she barely remained seated on the cold, hard edge of the tub. "I won't let it."

"Do you think you can protect all of them? That you can be in every place at once? Who will you let die and who will you protect? Kade? Maira? Brann?" There was a flash of gold in Ronan's blue eyes. "Maybe Rian, Crystal or Jasper. The Knights won't consider any of you human. Oh, they might try and use you, but you'll all be expendable and not trustworthy."

She couldn't remain seated. Rising to her feet, she glared at Ronan. "My grandfather is not to die."

"Ever?"

Amber opened her mouth to say never, but she couldn't keep the image of her grandfather from her mind. A dangerous man who'd killed a dragon while he'd been a prisoner. "What weapon did he use?"

Ronan frowned, then nodded once as his frown cleared. "None. He killed the dragon with his bare hands."

"Oh." Her legs felt weak. Wanting only to sit down again, she straightened her shoulders instead. "How is that possible?"

"Dragons have weaknesses, particularly when they're human. And Charles is cunning. Patient and very cunning."

"You sound like you admire him."

Ronan grinned, the predatory one that always made Amber dread what he was thinking. "He could almost be my human counterpart."

There was that sick feeling back in the pit of her stomach. "We get him back, then we decide what to do with him."

"Fight or negotiate."

"We can negotiate for him?"

"He's very valuable. I don't know if you'll have anything they'll want."

"Try negotiating first."

Ronan nodded once. "And you try and not get yourself killed before the end of the year."

"Yeah, I know. Someone's missing their home, sweet, home." She couldn't keep the bitterness from her voice.

"There's nothing sweet about it, but it's mine and I want it back." Ronan disappeared into the Void and Amber was left alone.

Sighing, she turned off the tap and sat on the edge of the bathtub. It was crazy. What was she supposed to do now?

"Amber?"

She mentally searched until she found Jasper in the lounge room. A little more searching showed her mother and Gary were out the back again. *"I'm in the bathroom."* Opening the door, she waited for her brother, closing the door behind him when he joined her.

"Why are you in here?"

She turned on the tap before she answered him. "Ronan was here." It didn't take her long before she'd filled him in on the visit.

"I've sorted Mum out and I'm going to go talk to Grandma next, but I don't have a clue what we're going to do about our grandfather."

Amber's gaze was drawn to the plaited leather band around Jasper's wrist, semi-precious stones down the centre of it, then to the silver rings on his fingers. Silver and semi-precious stones were what he worked with best for storing power. "Are they all full?"

"Yeah, but I'm not lit up like a Christmas tree." He nodded towards all the bracelets Amber wore, as well as her pendant and earring.

"Maybe you should be. I think we're going to need it."

"I can't believe our family. Bloody Knights. Of all the luck."

"If they hadn't been captured we wouldn't be in this mess."

Jasper shook his head. "No, it'd be worse. If they hadn't been captured, we'd have been Knights too and never known what it was like to be mages. Never flown as hawks and we wouldn't have captured our own castle. Or known dragons as anything other than enemies."

"Never have met Kade." That thought made her feel empty.

"Yeah." He fell silent.

Amber couldn't think of a single thing to say. Finally, she could. "What do we do with him?"

"I haven't got a clue, but he sounds like a real bastard."

"I can't believe Grandma has protected him all these years by hiding everything from us and quitting the Knights."

"Maybe she wasn't protecting him. Maybe it was Roger."

"I didn't think of that. It makes more sense. Not that much of this does make sense."

"Yeah, I know. I better go and see her. I'm only staying the day. I'm heading back in the morning."

"What did you tell Mum?" Amber didn't want to get their stories mixed up.

"The truth." Jasper grinned. "Mostly. I didn't mention Crystal. She'd probably feel obligated to tell her parents and they'd freak worse than Mum."

"What else didn't you mention?"

"Isleen, your house and our castle."

"So you didn't tell her much at all."

Jasper laughed. "When I left her, Gary was asking her if she wanted something to help calm her down."

"Great. Typical doctor. Always wanting to fill everyone with pills." She turned the tap off. "While you're at Grandma's, ask to look at the book she's got listing all the kill on sight dragons. And look at the crimes."

"All of them?"

"Until you think you're ready to throw the book at her."

"Okay." Jasper gave her a quick hug before he left.

Amber searched out her mother and Gary, shaking her head when she found them out the back. Making her way to the laundry windows, Amber watched her mother pace back and forth, Gary talking softly as Donna gestured wildly. It looked like her mother was still having problems with everything. Jasper wasn't as good as he thought he was.

Chapter Eight

It was late when Kade returned home and Amber was already in bed, trying unsuccessfully to sleep. She felt the mattress dip as Kade joined her in the king-sized bed. "Did you have any luck?"

"There were a couple that Maira and Rian were happy with. They'll give them a trial and see how they work out."

She snuggled against Kade when he finished getting comfortable. "Ronan found my grandfather."

"And?"

It took several minutes before she could bring herself to tell Kade everything. He remained silent once she'd finished. "Well?"

"I really don't know what to tell you, Amber."

"What would you do?"

"You shouldn't need to ask. Survival of the fittest."

She moved so she could rest her head on her hand,

her elbow propped up on the pillow. "You think I should kill him?"

"I think you shouldn't risk your life for someone you don't know and who is likely to want to kill you."

Sighing, Amber dropped back on her pillow. "Why has everything got to be so complicated?"

Kade reached for her, tugging her close. "This is your decision. He's your family. I'll help you with whatever choice you make."

"I-" she broke off, sitting up as she finally figured it out. "Damn it. Ronan thinks she's like me."

Kade sat up too. "What?"

"Mum. That she'll do anything for someone she loves. And he thinks Gary will follow his orders, but if he loves her too, all of Ronan's scheming might be for nothing."

"You sound happy about that."

"It'd serve him right if all his plotting and planning came to nothing." She reached for her mobile phone, which was on the bedside drawers.

"You're not going to ring him right now, are you? It's after midnight."

"Yep." She dialled Ronan's number, waiting for him to answer.

"This better be good."

"You think you can manipulate my mum through love."

"I know I can. If she loves him deeply enough she'll do anything for him. All you humans are the same."

"No, we're not."

"Did you figure out why yet?"

"Because you can't help plotting and planning?"

"Because she interferes in your plans through her ignorance. And that, in turn, interferes with mine."

"Can't you do anything for someone else for a change? Just for them with no benefits at all for you."

"No. There's no point to it." He hung up.

With a frustrated growl, Amber returned the phone to the bedside drawers. "You dragons are so annoying. Everything has to be complicated."

"Without complications, life would be boring."

"No it wouldn't," Amber muttered.

"Yeah, it would. Imagine a couple of hundred years of peace. What would you do with it?"

"Since I don't know what peace is like, how would I know?"

Kade laughed softly. "Get some sleep. Or at least be quiet so I can. It's been a long week with all the interviews I've held."

"I didn't know you'd been searching for warriors

that long. What made you think trouble was coming?"

"You attract trouble like magnets attract metal."

"I don't." Amber rolled over, her back to Kade as she lay on the edge of the bed, knowing he'd take up most of the space once he fell asleep and turned dragon. She didn't attract trouble. Or at least she never used to. Not until dragons came into her life.

* * *

Jasper had not long left for the city, and they were all seated at the kitchen table having lunch, when Ronan appeared out of the Void. "I've arranged a talk."

"What's going on," Donna demanded as Gary reached for her hand, which was resting on the table near her plate of sandwiches.

Ronan kept his gaze on Amber. "Be ready in an hour. No weapons allowed. Only the two of us can approach."

"What are we offering in exchange for him?"

"It doesn't matter right now. We're only talking and sounding them out. And meeting your grandfather."

"You'll see my father?" Donna leaned forward.

"Can Mum come too?" Amber asked.

"No. It's not a sight seeing trip," Ronan snapped.

"I haven't seen him since I was three-years-old."

Ronan ignored Donna, his gaze remaining on Amber. "Remember, no weapons allowed.

"Why only two?"

"Two of them, two of us. We meet on neutral grounds and then we'll discuss things. When the talks are ended, it's time to leave in a hurry. That's when the temporary truce is over."

"But they won't have any weapons."

Ronan shook his head. "Have I taught you nothing? A dragon without weapons is never truly unarmed."

"Neither am I." She could do more damage with claws and fireballs than she could with any weapon.

"One hour." Ronan returned to the Void, leaving arguments behind.

Amber tried to listen to what her mother had to say, but there wasn't a single word she could agree with. Rising to her feet, she kept her gaze on Donna. "No one else can go. I have to do this. It's the only way to keep us safe."

"You're a child. That man can't expect you to go wandering around the countryside without my permission," Donna said.

"Mum, it's settled. Things are different. I'm not a kid, I'm a Dragon Mage." She brought fire to one of her hands, snapping it closed to extinguish the flames a moment later.

"Being able to play with fire doesn't make you an adult," Donna said.

"I know. It's the people who want me dead that make me one." She regretted the comment the moment she saw her mother's expression. It had obviously been the wrong thing to say to convince her.

Donna rose to her feet. "We're leaving. I don't care where we go. Maybe England."

Amber laughed, a slightly brittle sound. "You don't get it, do you? There's nowhere far enough. Dragons go where they want." She made a sharp motion with her hand when Donna started to speak again. "I have to get ready." Striding from the kitchen, she headed for Kade's room, closing the door and leaning against it. Besides grabbing a jacket to throw on over her vest, there was nothing else she needed to do, other than not have to listen to another argument.

Hearing movement in the hallway outside, she tensed, relaxing when mentally searching the hallway showed her it was Kade. Half opening the door, she leaned against it, staring at him. "How safe is this?"

"Completely safe until it's over, but Ronan will get you out of there."

"Are you sure? How do you know that one day he won't decide that, word or not, he couldn't be bothered?"

"Because he'd be dead. Everyone now knows that you're his to protect. If you die and he's there, he'll be hunted until he's dead. It's our one law we all abide by."

"Bloody possessive dragons."

Kade grinned. "We keep what's ours or die trying."

"I miss my old life. It was so much simpler."

"I'm sorry. I didn't mean to drag you into all this, but I can't say I regret having you here with me."

Amber pushed away from the door, letting it swing completely open. She slid her arms around his waist, resting her head on his chest. "It'd be much better if someone wasn't always trying to kill us."

"We're dragons. We not only want to keep what's ours, but we want what's our neighbour's too."

Hearing footsteps, Amber mentally searched and found her mother was headed her way. Stepping back, she dragged Kade into the bedroom with her, closing and locking the door.

"What's wrong?"

"Mum's coming this way. I don't want any more

arguments. I just need a bit of peace and quiet before I meet my grandfather." A man who probably wanted her dead. As well as most of the people she cared about. She still didn't know what to do about him.

Kade linked his fingers through hers, leading her to the bed where he tugged her down to sit beside him. Wrapping an arm around her waist, he drew her close. "I wish I could be there with you, but the rules are two from each party negotiating."

"What can I expect?"

"It's a large open circular area about half a kilometre across. Even though you can leave through the Void from it, you can't enter it from the Void or speak to people in their minds. The paving stones prevent it."

"What are they made of?"

"Similar to Ronan's prison, but for some reason they not only prevent calls out, but also within."

"How?"

"I don't know. No one does. It could be the stone pillars that surround the place at intervals, but the only ones who'd know are the ones who built it and they all died centuries ago."

"Does it have a name?"

"*Feralenzi*. It's named after the dragon who first

suggested we needed a safe place for negotiations between enemies."

"And the dragons I'm meeting are my enemies?"

"They aren't your allies."

"But that doesn't mean they're enemies."

Kade laughed softly.

Amber lightly hit his chest with her open hand. "Oh shut up. Bloody dragons." Silence filled the room and Amber spent the time before Ronan arrived trying to think about what she could offer in exchange for her grandfather. Nothing came to mind. There was nothing she was willing to part with.

Ronan stepped out of the Void to stand at the foot of the bed. "Time to go."

Amber slowly rose to her feet, grabbing her jacket from the floor where she'd dropped it earlier. Shaking it out, she pulled it on. She turned to kiss Kade who'd joined her. "I'll be back soon."

Kade's hand lightly brushed across her cheek. "Be careful and get out of there as soon as the meeting is done."

Amber nodded, pulling away, her gaze still on him. She felt Ronan's hand land on her shoulder, his grip tightening. Then she was in the Void, her world reforming before her eyes as they stepped out of the

Void to arrive at Feralenzi. She was so not ready for this.

With a hand at the small of her back, Ronan guided her between two large pillars of glossy black stone. Beneath her feet were large uneven pavers, grass growing between the cracks. The place was empty of everything but the stone pillars that surrounded it, the whole space stretching out around them.

Directly opposite, six men stepped out of the Void. Three disappeared immediately while the other three started to cross the circle towards the middle of Feralenzi. Amber couldn't stop staring at the man in the middle. His hands were shackled in front of him, but his head was held high and his shoulders back, like he was the one in charge. Forty years of captivity hadn't weakened Charles' strength of character. Amber had a bad feeling that nothing would weaken this man. That he would never waver from his plan to eliminate all dragons.

They reached the centre of Feralenzi before the other group and Amber tested the area's security. Kade had been right. There was no mentally reaching anyone outside Feralenzi let alone in it. Anything spoken here would be heard by everyone in Feralenzi and there'd be no mentally calling for help. She fought the urge to step closer to Ronan. The last thing she should do was show weakness in front of the people who had finally reached the centre.

Ronan lightly touched his chest. "Ronan." He gestured to the side. "Amber."

The man opposite Ronan touched his own chest. "Blair." He gestured to the man next to him. "Charles." Then a little further across. "Irvin."

Both men were large, over six foot, and taller than Charles. Blair had swirling tattoos down both arms, bronze eyes and dark hair while Irvin had long blond hair tied back from his bearded face and green eyes with flecks of gold. They were dressed in black dragon-leather clothes. Long pants and vests.

"We have need of a captive from the Knights," Ronan said.

"You've already mentioned that, but you haven't said why," Irvin said.

"Why will not be discussed. You are obviously willing to part with your prisoner for the right price or you wouldn't be here," Ronan said.

While the three men spoke back and forth, making very little progress as far as Amber could see, she studied them. Why hadn't Ronan given her more information about them before they arrived? And why did he even need her here if there really wasn't anything she could do or say? She wondered if the bronze in Blair's eyes meant he was a Gold. Or the flecks of gold in Irvin's green eyes meant he was one too. Other than seeing them in dragon form, was there any way to tell? Alsandair's eyes were almost pure gold, but Kade's were only a golden brown so maybe the eyes didn't tell the full story. But, then if they were Gold, why had they needed someone to transport them through the Void? There was so much about dragons that she still didn't know.

Charles spoke, interrupting Amber's thoughts. "I knew a woman once with hair the colour of yours."

Amber struggled to come up with something to say. All she could think of was photos of her grandmother when she was younger, her hair the same rich chestnut waves that fell around her own shoulders. She shrugged. "It's a common enough colour."

"The woman I knew would never have let dragons speak on her behalf."

"People change. It's been forty years since you've seen family and friends," Amber said.

"If she has allied herself with dragons, that woman would be as dead to me as my son."

Had her grandfather just threatened her? Did he know who she was? She was conscious of the dragons watching her. "We aren't interested in your past, only how you can be of use to us in the future."

"I'm a worn out old man, no use to anyone."

"Quiet." Irvin hit Charles in the back and he lurched forward, barely keeping his feet. "He's valuable. If someone could break into his mind without destroying it, all the secrets of the Knights would be laid out for them."

"How many have tried?" Ronan asked.

"None with great experience. We are only a small clan," Blair said.

"A Goldless clan," Ronan said.

Anger flushed Irvin's face. "Our father is Gold."

"Yet none of his offspring or his grandchildren are." Ronan's tone remained even. "Your clan would dissolve if your father was to die."

Blair's hand reached for the empty scabbard at his side. "Is that a threat?"

Chapter Nine

Ronan shook his head. "Merely an observation."

"We are in negotiations for a Gold bride for one of our sons," Blair said. "Our situation isn't desperate and it has no bearing on these negotiations."

"I've heard that the Gold bride you've been wooing has many suitors to choose from. You have eight sons between you both, don't you?" Ronan asked.

"And a daughter," Blair said.

"What if I could provide a possible Gold bride for you?"

"We would want a guarantee," Irvin said.

"No guarantee. The raising of a female Gold and, if one of your sons could convince her when she is of age, a marriage," Ronan said.

Amber wanted to ask where Ronan would get a young Gold female. Then she realised, she had two in her keeping. She wanted to tell him no. Wanted to bring an end to the negotiations. But she couldn't, they had to maintain a united front. How long had he been planning this? Damn dragon couldn't stop plotting and planning and keeping secrets from her. It was an effort to keep her expression neutral and her body relaxed.

"You could guarantee we'd have the complete raising of her?" Blair asked.

Ronan shook his head. "No. There's likely to be conditions from the other party involved, but if you were willing to exchange your prisoner for the possibility of a Gold bride, I can start negotiations with the other party."

"We'll discuss this with our father," Irvin said.

"Shall we say this meeting is at an end?" Blair asked.

"Amber."

She met her grandfather's sharp blue eyes.

"I wish I could tell that woman that mourning is for the weak. The only emotion of value in these situations is revenge."

Revenge against who, she wanted to ask. Ronan spoke before she could think of a way to word her question.

"The meeting is ended." Ronan grabbed hold of Amber and took them away, through the Void.

She looked around at a bathroom she'd never seen

before. "Where are we? This isn't Kade's place. And I hope you weren't thinking about Doneele or Paili's egg when you were talking about brides. That isn't going to happen."

Ronan turned on a tap. "My place. And why isn't it going to happen?"

"You can't sell people."

"I'm not. They'll have complete freedom of choice."

"No." Amber glared at him.

Ronan shrugged. "Then I'll ask Jasper."

"No you won't. They're mine."

Ronan laughed. "So you can't sell people, but you can own them. How proud you make me feel of my teaching abilities at times. You're becoming more of a dragon every day."

Amber's anger evaporated as quickly as it had come and she was unable to meet Ronan's gaze. She didn't want to be a dragon. She wanted to be herself, not something Ronan made her. "They're not for sale."

"They would treat either one of them like a treasure. For that is what Gold bloodlines are. A treasure everyone wants. Without it, you can't rule."

"You seem to manage."

"No. Not where it matters. Without Gold you can

only ever be on the fringes of power. Only Gold can become a Representative or any rank higher."

"How would we know they'd treat them right? Doneele's parents were renegades, no one would want her if they knew."

"They won't know who her ancestors are. You claim her as your own and her past will be irrelevant. And you don't offer both of them. Only one. Never give more than you need to in a negotiation."

"How would we know?" Amber persisted.

"You could make it part of the conditions. Give them Paili's egg. She hasn't any attachment to you and won't know the difference. Come on Amber, I added in the conditions for you, the least you can do is consider it."

"It seems wrong." She wanted to pace, but there was no room.

"That's because you're looking at it as a human. See it through dragon eyes."

"How can I? I am a human."

Ronan's predatory smile appeared. "Are you?"

Amber pushed that disquieting thought away. "Yes." Her voice was firm, her gaze steady. "I'm human."

"Talk to Rian. He'll tell you this makes sense."

"I'd have to speak to Jay too. And probably Kade."

"You don't need to ask the entire world what they think. Your first warrior and your brother since they're in his care. That's more than enough."

Amber nearly smiled at the way Ronan spoke the words 'first warrior'. He'd told Rian he was an idiot not to give up that position now he co-owned land. "Maybe."

"It is." Ronan turned off the tap, stepped forward, grabbed Amber's wrist and took her through the Void before she had a chance to protest.

They emerged at the entrance of Temolae Keep, the castle Amber shared with Kade, Flinn, Rian, Crystal and Jasper. "What are we doing here?"

"Making a decision before too many people know what we're planning."

Jasper stepped out of the Void with Alsandair, who sent Amber a grin and a wink before he disappeared back into the Void. Jasper faced Ronan. "You do know I have other things to do than be at your beck and call."

"Alsandair's working for you again?" Amber asked Ronan.

Ronan pointed at Jasper. "No you don't." His finger moved towards Amber. "Is there something I should know?"

Amber shook her head. Ronan had been known to

kill those who annoyed him. She wasn't about to risk Alsandair's life. Not over a misunderstanding. "No. I was just surprised."

"Good. Rian will join us in the planning room." Ronan strode inside.

Jasper walked beside Amber. "What's going on?"

"I saw our grandfather."

"What's he like?"

"I think you're right. I'd say he's a real bastard."

"Amber!" Maira ran towards them, throwing her arms around Amber. "What are you doing here? I didn't believe it when one of the servants said you'd arrived."

"I need to speak to Rian." Amber returned her hug, missing Maira's vibrant personality. "When are you coming back to Australia?"

"Soon. These new warriors seem to be working out really well."

"We don't have all day," Ronan growled.

Amber held Maira a moment longer before she let her go. "Can you send a message to Kade to let him know where I am and that I shouldn't be too much longer."

"He doesn't know you're here?"

Amber shook her head, about to explain when Ronan grabbed her by the upper arm and marched her along the corridor. "I'll talk to you later," she threw over her shoulder. She turned on Ronan. "You can let me go now."

"When we're seated in the planning room."

Amber glared at Ronan, sparing a single daggered look for her brother who sniggered from behind her. When they reached the planning room, Rian started to cross the room, stopping when his father let her go.

"Are you fine?" Rian asked Amber.

She nodded, sitting at the large table in the middle of the room. "I need some advice."

Rian sat across from her. "What is wrong?" He sent a quick look in his father's direction.

Amber started to reassure Rian that his father wasn't the problem this time, but decided she didn't know that for certain. Instead, she told Rian and Jasper about the negotiation meeting.

"Not Doneele," Jasper said. "If you give them Doneele, Isleen will go with her."

"Oh Jasper, you're not." Amber stared worriedly at her brother.

"You can't talk. What about Kade?"

She started to argue, but Ronan cut her off. "Good. It's settled. Paili's egg will be used."

"Nothing has been decided," Amber said.

"I was thinking we should name her. We can't keep calling her the egg," Jasper said.

"No." Ronan slammed a hand against the table. "Name it and she," he gestured towards Amber, "will never want to part with it."

"Name the child, make the exchange," Rian said.

"What?" Amber couldn't believe Rian was siding with his father so quickly. "But we don't know they'll take care of her."

"I was thinking Topaz. There's an imperial topaz that's a golden orange colour and well…" Jasper's voice trailed off.

"Claiming her with a name linking her to you and your sister is a good strategy." Ronan nodded.

"I d–"

Amber kicked her brother who was sitting next to her. *"Shut up. Let him think what he wants. It makes you look stronger in his eyes."*

"I didn't think of that reason," Jasper told her.

"So?" Amber turned her attention to Ronan. "How do we protect Topaz?"

"Send a guardian with her," Rian said.

Jasper spoke at almost the same time. "Shared custody."

"Guardian?" Amber asked.

"Like Isleen is for Doneele," Rian explained before

he turned to Jasper. "What do you mean by shared custody?"

"We have Topaz for two weeks out of every thirteen."

"And if her guardian or Topaz complain about the way she's treated then she returns to our care," Amber said.

"Children always complain about their parents or those who raise them." Ronan sent a pointed look towards his son before his gaze returned to Amber.

"Complaints of mistreatment, force or harm. And it's her choice if she marries any of them. All they're getting is the chance to try and convince her one of them would make her a good husband," Amber said.

"It's settled then?" Ronan's gaze travelled around the table.

"Yes," Jasper said.

When Amber didn't answer, Ronan stared at her. "Well?"

"Are you sure Topaz will be safe?"

"With her bloodlines, she'll be adored, spoiled and treated like a queen. Paili came from a long line of Golds," Ronan said. "One of the purest lines."

Amber hesitated.

"She would be safer in their care than yours. They

would go to a great deal of trouble to protect her and woo her," Rian said to Amber.

She trusted Rian's advice a lot more than she trusted Ronan's. "Okay. It's settled."

Ronan rose from the table. "Finally. I'll return you home." His gaze moved from Amber to Jasper. "Alsandair will be here shortly to take you home." Looking at Amber again, he held out his hand.

"One moment," Rian said. "Have you seen Shannon? Her family sent a message here looking for her."

"No." Amber turned to her brother. "Jay?"

Jasper shook his head. "Haven't seen her in ages."

Ronan took Amber's arm. "Let me know if no one can find her."

Before Amber could protest, Ronan was taking her through the Void again and she found herself back at his place, in the bathroom. "What are we doing here? I thought you were taking me home."

He turned on the tap. "In a minute. Don't give your grandmother that message."

"I wasn't going to."

"Good. We don't need the Knights hunting us down.

In case Ronan still had someone watching her, she

decided to tell him her mother's threat. "Mum wants to take me to England. She wants to run and hide."

"And you think I wouldn't be able to find you?"

"I refused. I'm not going to spend my life running. If something's coming for me, I'll face it." She met his gaze, continuing to hold it when he remained silent, staring at her.

"I had a sister once." His words were quiet.

It took her a moment to recover from the shock to be able to speak. "Don't tell me I remind you of her."

"No. If she'd been more like you she might still be alive. She gave up too soon. Ran instead of facing what was after her." Ronan's gaze remained on her. "I'm starting to think you remind me of myself. Back when I was young and had no clue. Only my wits and determination not to be the next casualty."

Amber bit back her instinct to argue, reminding herself she'd once told him something similar. "I've always seen the similarities."

Ronan's predatory smile emerged. "I know. But I don't think you were looking at the correct ones." He turned off the tap before he held out his hand. "Ready to return to your Gold?"

Amber nodded and soon found herself on Kade's doorstep, Ronan disappearing into the Void. She mentally searched the house, wincing when she found her mother and Gary in the lounge room. She was tempted to go around to the back door, but steeling herself for a lecture, she opened the door and stepped inside.

Chapter Ten

A noise drew Amber from sleep and she sat up, fire pooling in her hands. Beside her, Kade turned human.

"If I'd been an assassin, one of you would have been dead." Ronan stood at the foot of the bed, looking down at them.

Amber extinguished the fire in her hands, checking the time on her phone. "It's not quite three a.m. What are you doing here? I've got school in the morning."

"It's all been arranged. I've sent Chait to collect the egg."

"Topaz." Amber rose from the bed, glad that these days she wore dragon-leather to sleep in. Life was too chaotic to do otherwise.

"They've agreed to all conditions." Ronan withdrew a scroll, holding it out.

While Amber took the scroll, Kade turned on the

light. Together they sat on the edge of the bed and read through the details. Amber rolled it back up and held it out to Ronan.

"Are you happy with it?" Ronan took the scroll, tucking it inside his vest.

"Yes."

"When we arrive, we'll all sign two copies, one for each side to hold. Then we'll make the exchange. They've agreed we can bring someone to carry the egg if they can bring someone to receive the egg."

Amber reached for Kade's hand. "So they're going to let Kade come with us?"

Ronan nodded. "They agreed. He's to take Charles straight to my house the moment the exchange has been made."

"What about us?" Amber asked.

It was Kade who answered her. "You can't leave until the meeting has ended and both sides say the meeting is finished. This way, what is exchanged can be taken to safety before the truce is over."

"That makes sense." A light knock on the bedroom door ended any further comments Amber would have made and she mentally searched the corridor. "Come in, Chait."

He entered the room, the egg cradled close to his chest, his gaze on Amber. "Jasper said for you to make sure Topaz is safe and to be careful." He handed the egg to Kade.

Amber nodded, turning off her phone and slipping it into her pocket. She didn't want to risk offending anyone with a ringing phone during the truce.

"Time to go." Ronan pointed a finger at Kade. "And make sure you take Charles straight to my house. I have warriors waiting on the rooftop garden to stop him from trying to escape."

"I'm not simple," Kade said.

Amber stepped between them. She'd spent yesterday umpiring as Ronan showed Kade the path through the Void from Feralenzi to his house, making Kade practice repeatedly in case Blair and Irvin agreed they could bring an extra person. "I'm ready." Well, about as ready as she was ever likely to be. She held her hand out to Ronan.

He took her hand and they passed through the Void to Feralenzi, Kade stepping out of the Void only a moment after them. Amber let go of Ronan's hand, taking a deep breath as she walked forward, Kade on one side, Ronan the other. They were nearly half way to the centre when six figures appeared outside the pillars, two disappearing to leave the other four to cross Feralenzi.

Amber couldn't help staring at her grandfather. He

didn't look any different, still the same arrogant man. Reaching the centre, she stopped between Ronan and Kade, waiting for the other party to reach them. When they did, Ronan and Blair exchanged scrolls and each read them over before the signing began. Once the four of them had signed, Ronan and Blair returned the scrolls to their vests.

Ronan gestured Kade forward. "Topaz. Paili's unborn Gold daughter. Captured in battle and never claimed by her mother's clan."

"You are certain it is a Gold female?" Blair asked.

"Without a doubt," Ronan said.

"It would be useful to learn how you know this. Others would find it helpful."

"The one who can tell this is costly and a recluse," Ronan said.

Amber mentally shook her head at Ronan's lies. It was a wonder he even knew what a truth was with how many lies he continually spoke. Although some days she would probably prefer to be a recluse.

The other man with the two brothers pushed Charles forward, stopping in front of Kade. He held out his hands, taking the egg and disappearing at the same time as Kade grabbed hold of Charles' arm and entered the Void.

Ronan held out a hand. "The key for the shackles."

Irvin handed it over. "I doubt you'll ever want to use it. The old man is dangerous."

Ronan pocketed the key. "The guardian we chose for Topaz should be at your castle by the time you return there. We'll be back here in eleven weeks to collect Topaz for our two weeks."

Blair and Irvin both nodded, only Blair spoke. "We will have her here along with your guardian and the guardian we have chosen. Shall we call this meeting ended?"

"The meeting is over." Ronan reached for Amber. Before his hand could make contact, balls of fire, ice and lightning hit him all at once.

Blair and Irvin made a run for the edge of Feralenzi where two men came out of the Void, running towards them.

Four dragons swooped out of the air, humans on their backs attacking with mage power. Amber grabbed hold of Ronan who roared as he was bombarded with more fire, ice and lightning. They entered the Void, and Amber barely managed to hold onto Ronan as he shifted to dragon form, letting go of him the moment they left the Void.

She backed away from him as he roared, fire erupting from his mouth. Around them people shouted and Amber tried to figure out where they were. She didn't have a clue. Ronan roared again and this time he struck out at her. Remembering how crazy it had made Rian to be forced into dragon shape from mage attacks, Amber turned into a goshawk, taking to the sky.

Ronan chased her, flames streaking past her. Ahead she saw the shoreline and she figured out their location. Ronan's lands. The ones still held by his enemy. Behind Ronan streamed a group of dragons and Amber screeched, flying faster. She had to do something.

Mentally reaching out to Ronan didn't help. She found only a wild, crazed creature like a wyvern. He needed to be healed. That had helped Rian. But Rian hadn't been hit so many times. Behind them the other dragons were closing the gap. If she was going to do something to get them out of this mess, it had to be fast.

There was only one thing she could do. Holding back her fear, Amber angled away, coming up above Ronan. When he caught sight of the other dragons, instead of trying to continue chasing her, he headed for them. Mentally swearing, Amber dived for his back, becoming human and gripping him tightly. He roared again, rolling to throw her off. She barely managed any healing before she was tumbling through the sky, frantically trying to become a goshawk again.

Then her wings were beating and the ground was receding and Ronan was once again chasing her. She led him away from the other dragons, continuing along the coastline, wishing she had help. There wasn't even time to count how many dragons chased them, but there had to be at least a dozen. Reaching for Ronan's mind, she found he was still as crazed as before. She needed to try again.

As soon as she felt they'd put enough distance between the other dragons, Amber angled around, coming in above Ronan. Once again he took off after the other dragons and she dived for his back. She managed to heal him more than last time before he dislodged her. Falling towards the ground, she desperately tried to change, exhaustion sapping her energy.

"Amber!" Ronan arrowed towards her, his claws grabbing hold of her as he dragged them into the Void.

They crashed into hard rock as they came out and the wind was knocked from her. Ronan turned human, landing beside her, his natural form visible. She stared at him, trying to breathe again. He was slightly shorter than usual, more muscular and looked as young as his son Rian. His hair had lightened to a white blond and his pale blue eyes were flecked with gold.

When she no longer fought for breath, she asked, "Where are we?" She tried to move, but nausea swamped her and pain exploded in her head.

"The caves along the coastline. I couldn't take us far." Ronan struggled to sit up.

She stayed still, barely able to focus on Ronan's words from the pain. Hopefully it would hurt less to stay still. She tried to think what to do, but pain and exhaustion made it hard. The pounding in her head made her think she might have struck it when they'd landed. "Will they find us in here?"

"Let's hope not." Ronan leaned against the cave wall. "We need to find Shannon."

"I can't believe she broke her word and made Dragon Mages." Amber winced as she breathed too deep. Maybe there was a broken rib or two. As soon as her head stopped swimming enough for her to focus, she'd heal herself.

"Are you hurt?"

"When I catch my breath, I'll heal myself."

"What did you think you were doing?"

"When?" Couldn't he shut up? He was making her head pound worse.

"I was distracted by the other dragons. You could have easily gone."

She was about to demand why he was so angry with her. Didn't she just save his life? Then it hit her. She'd saved his life. Again. "I don't know where we are. I have no idea how to get from your lands to anywhere else."

"You're saying you saved me to ask for directions."

Amber glared at him, trying to focus. Pain made it nearly impossible. It was difficult trying to come up with a plausible explanation. Her head spun with pain and blacking out was a distinct possibility. "Who else was I going to ask? The dragons that looked like they wanted to kill us?"

"This incessant need to save everyone around you will get you killed eventually," Ronan warned.

Amber had no idea what she could say to that comment without angering him further. She fought overwhelming exhaustion and pain.

"I can smell blood. How badly are you hurt?"

She gingerly touched her chest, feeling a damp stickiness. "Ahh crap." Maybe she'd have to heal herself before she could think clearly. Hopefully she didn't make a mess of it. Pressing her hands against the wound, she tried to focus.

"Amber?"

Looking up, she saw Ronan peering down at her, his eyes seeming to have more gold flecks in them than last time. His image swam before her eyes as she figured out how to make the bleeding stop, knitting together two of her broken ribs. Exhaustion swamped her and everything went completely black.

Chapter Eleven

When Amber came to, her head was resting on Ronan's lap and he leaned against the cave wall again. "Ronan?"

He looked down at her.

This time she was almost certain his eyes were different. "What have you been doing?"

"Sitting here waiting for you to wake up."

"No. Your eyes. Is there more gold in them?"

"You think? I wasn't sure."

"What have you been doing?" She asked him again.

"Rest, kitten. Better yet, is there any power in these?" He lifted her arm, the bracelets jangling together. "It'd be nice to get out of here before night falls."

"It's nearly night?" She struggled to sit up, gasping at the pain.

"Stay still. You've got at least three broken ribs and who knows how many other problems."

"We have to go home. Everyone will be worried."

"They'll have to remain worried. I can't take us that far yet."

Amber closed her eyes, assessing the damage. It seemed like the broken ribs were the worst of it. Drawing energy from her bracelets, she focused on one of her ribs, straightening and fusing it together, a sharp indrawn breath at the pain that radiated through her. By the time she'd healed herself, half her gold bracelets were empty. She'd been a lot worse than she'd thought. A pity she hadn't been thinking clearly enough earlier to draw some of the stored power. But she'd been in too much pain.

"If you give me a minute, I'll heal you." She drew power from a couple more bracelets, thinking it was going to take her ages to store all that power again. There was no way she was going to bring herself to the point of exhaustion to fill them quickly. With the way life currently was, that wouldn't be safe.

A few minutes later, she finished healing Ronan, feeling exhausted even after she'd drawn more power from her jewellery. Ronan changed before her eyes, becoming older, his gold flecked eyes turning pale blue and his hair darkening. "We can leave whenever you're ready."

Ronan stared at her silently. Several minutes passing before he spoke. "I don't believe you. Especially since you could have got directions from anyone."

Amber leaned against the wall beside him, wishing he'd let it go. "And risk having my throat slit?"

"I thought you said you were going to tell me the truth."

Amber grinned. "Maybe I lied."

"Amber." There was a warning in his voice.

She had to make it good and something he could understand. Something that had at least some truth about it. "You've said yourself that you're the oldest dragon in existence."

"I am."

"Then you're obviously doing something right."

"I don't have all day for your explanation."

"You never break your word so that makes you my only ally I can truly trust. If you die, who can I turn to for help when I need it? No one else has your experience."

"That's true. The younger generations are nothing like the dragons of my generation."

Amber sat up so she could meet his gaze. "Why did you give me that power over you?"

"If I disappear for a while, survival of the fittest will take care of you soon enough."

She smiled slightly, mentally searching for him. The tug was strong, like a rope tied between them. She strengthened it like she'd recently done with Kade, Crystal and Jasper in the hope she'd always be able to find them, no matter where they were. "I could probably find you."

"Possibly."

"You never have only one reason for what you do. You're far more complicated than that."

Ronan's predatory smile formed. "I've outlived everyone. No matter what happens, I manage to survive it. One day, your Gold will die too and I'll be there to take his place."

Fear struck at Amber, wiping the smile from her face. "No! It's not going to happen. I'm not going to let him die."

Ronan shrugged. "Things happen."

She pointed a finger at him, an accusation in her tone. "You're not to harm him. We have a deal."

"I won't need to do anything. Life is precarious. Survival of the fittest, remember?"

"He will survive."

"Maybe, but other gambles of mine have paid off."

"All of them?"

"Not all, but enough." He rose to his feet. "It's time to go." He held a hand out to her.

Amber struggled to her feet, ignoring his hand. "He's mine and I won't let anything happen to him." A fierce, protective feeling filled her.

Ronan wrapped his hand around her upper arm, his predatory smile forming. "I love it when you sound like a dragon, kitten." He took them into the Void, bringing them out into his house.

Noise erupted around them, warriors all talking at once. Kade raced across the room to Amber and held her tight.

"I smell blood." He pulled away so his hands could roam her limbs, checking for injuries.

"I'm fine now." She grabbed his hands, stepping in close to him. "What about Charles?"

"He's lucky he's still alive," Kade growled.

"What happened?"

"He tried to escape, wounded several dragons and broke some furniture."

"Amber." Jasper came into the room. "You better ring Mum. She's been calling every half an hour."

She swore, pulling away from Kade to draw her

phone from her pocket and turn it on. "What have you told her?"

"We couldn't tell her anything. You went to make the exchange and neither of you returned. Chait went to Feralenzi and said it looked like there'd been a battle. Are you okay?" His gaze went from her head to toes then arrowed in on her chest. "Is that blood?"

"I'm fine." She dialled her mother's number.

Donna answered immediately. "Amber, is that you? Are you okay? What happened? Talk to me."

"Give me a chance."

"What happened?"

"We were attacked-"Amber nearly groaned when her words set her mother off. "Mum. Mum." She gritted her teeth as she listened to how worried her mother had been and how she was never going to let Amber do anything like this ever again. "Mum!"

"Come home, Amber. I can't go through another day like this."

"Later. I need to see my grandfather first."

"And what about me? I haven't seen my father since I was three-years-old."

"I'll see what I can organise. I have to go, Mum." But it took her several attempts and promising she'd return that night before Donna finally let her go. Sighing heavily, Amber returned the phone to her pocket, glancing around the now nearly empty room. "Where'd Ronan go?"

Kade shrugged. Jasper pointed towards the doorway.

Amber reached for Ronan with her mind. Locating him, she headed through the house, Kade and Jasper on her heels. She took a couple of wrong turns, only because her body couldn't go straight through walls like her mind could, but she arrived in time to see Ronan hit Charles.

"Enough!" Amber strode into the room, glaring at Ronan.

"He injured my warriors." Ronan met her glare with narrowed eyes.

"You better have somewhere else to keep him. He's not staying in this prison." It was the same room Daray had been held in when he'd been interrogated. There was still only a single stool bolted to the ground. "He's my grandfather."

"Do you claim him after all?" Ronan asked.

She still didn't know if she did. How could she? He was a stranger to her. A dangerous stranger who probably wanted her boyfriend dead. "Treat him well or I'll be forced to."

Ronan stared at her a little longer, before he inclined his head. "I'll organise a bed and some heavy furniture he can't lift and use as a weapon. But he will remain shackled and chained to a bolt so he can't attack whoever visits him."

"Okay." She turned to her grandfather, moving closer to look at the battered man, unable to prevent herself from reaching out to heal him. He stepped back before she could touch him.

Jasper joined her. "Does he know?"

She shrugged, meeting the sharp blue eyes that watched her. "We're your daughter Donna's children."

"Better than if you were Roger's children." Charles' gaze remained on Amber, but he nodded towards Jasper. "Is he a mage too?"

Jasper answered. "Yes."

"Then I have no grandchildren. All five of you are dead to me."

Ronan spoke from behind Amber. "He disowned you, now will you drop all ideas of claiming him?"

Amber ignored Ronan. "Dragons and humans are the same. We fight, love, hate, help, kill, have families. We're all the same."

"No. Not even close. They don't belong in this world. It isn't theirs. They think that because they have the power to walk between worlds they can wander where they wish. They can't. This is our world and they have no place in it."

Amber grinned at her grandfather. "Now there's a dragon comment if ever I heard one." She looked over her shoulder to Ronan who leaned against the wall, Kade not far from him. "Maybe it isn't your teaching after all. It might just be in my blood." Her relief was short lived, destroyed as she recalled all the dragons her grandfather had killed and remembered her battle with Paili.

"I'm nothing like a dragon," Charles snarled.

Jasper shook his head. "Our family is so screwed up. Good thing Mum's dating a shrink."

"Please, let's not go there," Amber said wearily.

"Gary's not too bad."

"What's Dad think about him?" Her gaze remained on Charles even though her question was directed to Jasper.

"I haven't got a clue. We had a bit of a falling out."

Amber spun to face her brother. "What? Why? And when did this happen?"

"Monday. The bitch he's been dating let it slip that they've been together a lot longer than Dad let on."

"He was seeing her behind Mum's back?"

Jasper nodded.

Amber rubbed at her forehead. "I can't think about

that right now." She gestured towards Charles. "What are we going to do with him?"

"Lock him up and throw away the key?" Jasper asked.

"The first sensible suggestion I've heard all day," Ronan said.

"Do you really want your grandfather held by Ronan? We could transport him to Temolae Keep. Rian is currently preparing a cell in case we need it," Kade said directly to Amber.

"I don't know. Let me know when it's ready." Out loud, Amber said, "I don't think it's time for that yet. Besides, Mum wants to see him."

Jasper gestured to all of Charles. "Like this? Do you really think she'll tolerate her father being kept prisoner?"

"What would you do if we set you free?" Amber met her grandfather's gaze again.

"Return to my wife. Did you give Helen my message?"

Amber shook her head. "I won't carry messages of hate and revenge for you."

"So if I asked you to tell her I love her and miss her, then you'd pass that on."

"Yes."

Charles stared at her for nearly a minute. "Then tell

her I have never forgotten our wedding day and have always remained true to the vows we made to each other. The only regret I have is that we never had the chance to raise our son as a true Knight."

"Okay."

"You will pass that along?"

"Amber." There was a warning in Ronan's tone.

She ignored it. "Yes."

Charles inclined his head. "Maybe there is some shred of humanity left in you after all."

Anger exploded in Amber and it took all her willpower to hold back the panther. "I am human. And you and everyone else can stop suggesting otherwise." She spun on her heel, striding from the room, Kade following. She was nearly outside, when Kade pulled her to him, holding her tight. "I am human," she muttered.

"I know."

She looked up at him. "Do you?"

He smiled. "A little crazed maybe, but still human." He rested his nose against her cheek, inhaling deeply. "You still smell mostly human. A faint touch of dragon and goshawk and a strong dose of panther, but I think that's only because you're close to changing. Normally it's only a slight smell of panther."

"That doesn't sound very human to me."

"Of course it does."

Amber pulled away from him. "I need to see my grandma before we go back to your place."

"You want to go now?"

"One minute." She reached for her brother with her mind. *"Are you right to get home or should I organise something?"*

"Let me check." There was a lengthy pause. *"I'm right. Are you going?"*

"Yeah. I'll drop in and see Grandma first."

"That'll be fun."

"Won't it." She linked her fingers through Kade's, wondering if she should say goodbye to Ronan. No, she didn't need any lectures from him. "We can go now."

It took only moments for him to use the Void, to take her to Helen's house. They arrived on her balcony, the location Kade was most familiar with.

Stepping inside, she looked back at Kade who remained in the doorway. "I won't be long."

"I'll be here if you need me." He crossed the room and dropped onto the bed.

Chapter Twelve

Amber's steps slowed as she crossed the room. The last thing she wanted to do was see her grandmother, but if she put it off, she'd probably never get around to delivering the message. It was kind of sweet and something she hadn't expected of the old man. And telling her he'd remained faithful to his wife was sappy, but also really nice. She searched ahead, finding her grandmother in the lounge room.

When she reached the lounge room doorway, she stopped to watch her grandmother as she sat in front of the television, dozing in an armchair. Helen jerked awake, looking in her direction, her gaze narrowing.

"What do you want?" She rose to her feet.

"I have a message from your husband."

"You've seen him?"

She hesitated. Telling her grandmother that her

husband was her prisoner didn't seem like the best idea. "Yeah."

"What did he say?"

Amber closed her eyes for a second, trying to recall the exact words. "He said to tell you he hasn't forgotten your wedding day and he remained true to you. Ahh, the vows you made. And he regrets not being able to raise your son together."

"That's it?" Helen looked like she didn't believe her.

"Maybe I should have recorded it. He mentioned your wedding day. Your vows and being faithful to them and your son." Frowning, she marked each point off on a finger. "Oh, and wanting to train him as a true Knight."

"A true Knight."

Amber nodded. "Yes. He regrets not being able to raise your son as a true Knight." Helen seemed to shrink before her eyes, dropping into the armchair. "Grandma? Are you okay?"

"Where is he?"

"Ah, he's still a prisoner."

Helen nodded, her gaze distant. She eventually looked up at Amber. "Go. You've delivered your message."

"Are y-"

"Go." Helen's voice was stronger this time.

Amber's jaw tightened as she turned away, heading for her bedroom. "Ungrateful old bitch," she muttered. She was halfway up the stairs when guilt hit her. She'd just given her grandmother the first words from her husband in forty years. Of course she was going to be hurting. She mentally searched for her grandmother, surprised to find she was now in her bedroom. Quietly heading back to the lounge room, her steps slowed as she approached the bedroom door. She really hoped Helen wasn't in tears because there was no way she'd want anyone to see that. Amber listened, trying to figure out what Helen was doing before she interrupted.

"Put me through to the High Protector. I have some important information for him."

"Kade!" Amber raced across the lounge room, bursting into her grandmother's room.

"This is Hel–"

Ripping the cordless phone from her grandmother, Amber disconnected the call, throwing the phone into the lounge room behind her. "What do you think you're doing?"

"Amber?" Kade arrived behind her.

"What's he doing here?" Helen pointed past Amber, at Kade.

"Is that what it was? A message to get in touch with the Knights?"

Helen smiled. "Not very clever, are you?"

"Then why don't you explain it to me?"

"Amber, what's going on?"

"She tried to ring the Knights." Then aloud to Helen. "I'm waiting."

"Our wedding vows included avenging each other if dragons should capture or kill us."

"And the bit about being a true Knight?"

"If one can't ever be a true Knight, then they have turned to the dragon's side."

Amber swore. She didn't have a clue what she was going to do with her grandmother, but she couldn't leave her there to tell the Knights about Kade. There was no way she was going to risk getting him killed. "So that's it? Forty years of silence and you'll break it because of one obscure comment? Your husband is still a prisoner."

"It was never about Charles. He always knew the risks and willingly accepted them. It was for Roger. He was a child. It wasn't his choice. He was born to this and never got the chance to decide. That choice was stolen from him."

"He's married with three daughters. The oldest is Gold," Kade said.

"You dragons ruin everything you touch. Everything." There was a wealth of bitterness in Helen's voice. "I kept quiet. They said if I kept quiet and never hunted another dragon he'd be safe. That isn't safe. Making him a dragon was never meant to be a part of it."

"It was his choice. They never allowed him to marry his wife. The two of them eloped," Kade said.

"Because they twisted his mind so he didn't know any better."

Amber stepped out of the doorway, not wanting to hear any more. She had to figure out what to do. Slowly walking across the lounge room, she took out her phone, dropping into the armchair her grandmother had been sitting in. The television was still on, an ad playing.

Staring at her phone, she could hear Helen and Kade talking. Kade's tone even, Helen's full of bitterness. What was she meant to do? Reunite her grandparents? She swore again, dialling Ronan's number.

Ronan took several rings to answer. "He's still safe. I haven't ripped his heart out if that's what you were wondering."

"What size bed did you put in the room?"

"King. I thought it might be a little hard for him to

use one that size as a weapon." When Amber didn't say anything, Ronan spoke again. "What's wrong now?"

Admitting a failure to Ronan was harder than she thought it would be. "It was a message to ring the Knights."

"That was always a possibility."

"Why didn't you say something?"

"I tried. You ignored me."

She bet he enjoyed pointing that out to her. And it wasn't like he'd tried very hard. "I thought maybe we could keep them together for now."

"And give them a chance to plot something?"

"Can you quit being annoying and come and get her? I need to be home tonight and at this rate I'll be lucky to make it before midnight."

"I'll be on your balcony in a second." Ronan disconnected.

Amber put her phone away and stood, about to join Kade. The argument between him and Helen was getting worse and Amber changed her mind, heading for the stairs. She reached the bottom as Ronan arrived at the top.

"Is there anyone who'll notice her gone?"

Amber shrugged. "I don't know. Mum will. I don't know how I'm going to explain it to her."

"That she rushed to her husband's side?" Ronan reached the bottom step.

"This is so complicated. What would you do?"

Ronan's predatory smile formed. "Rip all the information from their minds that I can and kill them."

"Don't even try," Amber warned.

He shrugged. "You asked what I'd do."

"They're my grandparents. Would you have done the same to yours?" She shook her head. "What am I thinking? You probably would. After all, didn't you eat the heart of one of your sons?"

"If my grandparents had wanted me dead, I would have killed them before they could've killed me. Why do you persist in treating your enemies as trusted allies?"

"They're not my enemy. They're family!"

"Family who want you dead."

She stepped back from him as if struck. "She's my grandma." Her voice sounded small and lost.

Ronan advanced on her. "Do you want to know who my first kill was? It was my uncle."

She held her ground. "Why?"

"My sister screamed for me in my mind, begging me to help her. I told her I was coming, but still she ran instead of standing and facing him. Ran straight into the trap he'd set for her. Then he came for me. I was all that stood between him and the land he wanted."

"What about your parents?"

"He'd already killed them. My sister found them, my mother's heart ripped out and missing, my father only recognisable by the ring he wore. I waited for him. Waited for Emlyn. He came with the sunrise, two of his warriors with him. And I killed them all. His was the first heart I took. So don't you tell me about family. I know all about them. They can kill you as easily as another and stab you in the back just as quick."

"I'm sorry."

"I don't want your human sympathy. You want to give me sympathy, give me dragon sympathy."

"And what is that?"

"Revenge." There was a flash of gold in his pale blue eyes.

Amber reached out to rest her hand on his shoulder. "I've already promised to help you get back your lands."

"Then don't get yourself killed before you've fulfilled that promise." He looked past her. "I'll take the Knight to her husband. If she's to be in the same room as him it'll be in chains too."

Amber hesitated, then nodded. "Okay."

Ronan stepped past her.

Amber's hand fell to her side and she hurried after him, worried about their first meeting.

Helen broke off mid sentence to point at Ronan. "You!" Grabbing a sword from beside her bedroom door, she ran towards Ronan, swinging it at him. "Murderer."

Ronan leapt out of the way and still Helen came at him, expertly swinging the sword. Kade rushed her from behind and Ronan disarmed her while Kade struggled to hold the wildly flailing woman.

"Grandma. Enough. Please stop or you'll get hurt," Amber pleaded.

"Traitor." Helen glared at her.

"He's going to take you to your husband."

"Make me a prisoner you mean," Helen snapped.

"I'm sorry. But you want me dead. What am I meant to do?"

"I want the dragons dead. If you help us fight them, the Knights would have a use for you."

Amber stared silently at her grandmother. Her glasses were crooked, Kade still held her arms pinned at her sides and she sent daggered looks to Ronan. Had she ever known this woman? It didn't seem like it. "I'll come and see you tomorrow after school." Her words were soft, exhaustion making her want to curl up in bed and pull the blankets over her head for a week. Instead, she kept her gaze steady and her stance firm. "No one will harm you if you cooperate."

"I'd rather die," Helen spat.

"That can be arranged," Ronan said.

Amber faced Ronan. "She's mine."

"Are you sure you don't want to think about this one too?" Ronan gestured towards Helen.

"No. She's mine. Until she's coming at me with a blade, she's mine."

Ronan raised an eyebrow. "But it's okay for her to come at me with a blade?"

Amber couldn't help laughing. "Are you afraid of a little old lady, Ronan?"

"No, but she better be afraid of me if she goes for you with a blade, Amber. Because you've just given me permission to kill her if she does."

"Traitor!" The word was filled with anger and bitterness, cutting off Amber's protests.

She looked from her grandmother to Ronan, with a glance at Kade who steadily watched her, still keeping Helen's arms pinned. Was Ronan right? Would her grandmother kill her if she got the chance? Once she would have said no. Actually, she probably would have said hell no. Now she didn't have a clue. Giving a curt nod Amber met Ronan's gaze. "Take her to her husband." It hurt to speak the words in the emotionless tone she used, but not as much as the thought that her grandmother might want to kill her.

Ronan returned her nod with an equally curt one, grabbing Helen from Kade and disappearing into the Void.

Amber didn't care if Golds were watching her from the Void, her legs couldn't hold her up anymore. She dropped onto the ground, her hands covering her face as she tried to figure out what she'd done.

Kade wrapped his arms around her, lifting her up. "I'll take you home."

Pulling her hands from her face, she stared up at him. "I can't face another lecture from my mum."

"You won't have to. I can take us straight to my room."

"How about the bathroom? I can't sleep coated in blood, sweat and dirt."

"No. I can't manage that yet. You'll have to shower here." Kade took them to her balcony through the Void.

Once Amber had showered and changed into fresh dragon-leather clothes, he took her to his room where she collapsed on the bed, falling instantly asleep.

Chapter Thirteen

Standing at the bathroom sink in Kade's house, Amber filled another bracelet with her power. She'd filled three before school and now she'd filled another two. It wasn't enough. There were still eight that were empty, but she didn't want to exhaust herself. Especially not before she saw her grandmother. Who knew what she'd face.

There was a knock on the bathroom door. "Gary sent me a text to say your mother has finished packing a bag for your grandmother and they're on their way back. If you still want to leave before she returns and realises you're not taking her to see her parents, we better go now."

Sliding the bracelet on, Amber opened the bathroom door and stared at Kade. She really didn't want to take him anywhere near her grandparents. That just didn't seem like a good idea. But she doubted he'd be willing to stay away. "Okay, let's get out of here before I get my second lecture for the day." She'd been greeted with one over breakfast since she'd slept through the opportunity last night. Pulling out her phone, she turned it off so she didn't get any irate calls from her mother while she was with her grandparents, then slid it into her pocket. Her mother would ring the moment she found out the bag she'd packed would be collected by one of Ronan's Golds and she wouldn't get to see her parents, particularly her father.

Chuckling, Kade wrapped an arm around her, taking her to Ronan's place through the Void. He was there to meet them.

Amber stepped away from Kade. "How are they?"

"Alive."

She rolled her eyes at Ronan's answer. "You haven't messed with their heads, have you?"

"Not yet."

"Then don't. I wouldn't want them broken." She walked beside Ronan, Kade following.

"Then maybe you should see what information you can get out of them," Ronan said.

"Don't mess with them. I was the one who gave up Topaz for him and Grandma is mine."

"Until she attacks you with a blade."

Amber had no reply so she fell silent, thankful when they reached the room her grandparents were kept in.

Ronan swung the door open, stepping in first, his gaze taking in the room before he stepped to the side and let Amber enter. "As I said." He gestured towards the elderly couple sitting on the edge of the large timber bed. "Both alive."

They rose to their feet, Helen coming forward as far as her chain allowed her. "Have you told Donna what you've done?"

"I told her you're staying with your husband."

"Did you tell her you had me imprisoned? That her father is still imprisoned. Traitor!"

"Stop calling me a traitor," Amber yelled.

"You've sided with the dragons against us. You're a traitor," Helen spoke equally as loud.

"I didn't even know the Knights existed."

"That's their fault." Helen pointed at Ronan. "Murderer." She spared a glare for him before she continued to glare at Amber. "How could you side with someone who's killed your own relatives?"

Amber felt Kade move to stand behind her and she felt safer. She didn't have to do this alone. She lowered her voice, trying to remain calm, but the panther let her know she was nowhere near calm.

"The pair of you would run straight to your Knights if I set you free."

Helen shook her head. "No, we'd take the time to kill your dragons first."

Amber's voice rose again. "So what am I meant to do? Let you kill the person I love?"

"He's a dragon, not a person."

Kade stepped to the side of Amber so he could look at her. *"The first time you tell me you love me you yell it at someone else? Not much of a romantic, are you?"*

Amber sent him a glare. *"Better than not telling anyone at all."*

Kade slowly smiled, closing the gap between them. *"I won't be telling you here, in the middle of an argument with your grandparents."*

Amber ignored her grandmother's demands to know what Kade was saying to her. "Can we deal with this later?"

Kade reached out to rest his hands on her hips. "No." He pulled her tight against him, his lips meeting hers as he took her through the Void.

Amber pulled away from him to look around, unable to recognise where he'd brought them. "I was in the middle of talking to my grandparents." She mentally searched the area, finding both Rian and Maira in the building. "We're at Temolae Keep?"

"Yeah. Our room."

Amber looked around. There were two closed doors, an oversized bed in the centre, a tall chest of drawers on the wall opposite the foot of the bed and smaller drawers on either side of the bed. She returned her attention to Kade. "You can't just drag me off like that. What was wrong with asking?"

"You would have said no. Now how about you try that earlier statement and you don't yell it at someone else."

She struggled to hold onto her annoyance at him for dragging her away from her argument. The smile that wanted to escape let her know it was a losing battle. "I'm not sure which statement you want me to repeat. There were so many things I was yelling."

Kade reached for her, sliding his hand behind her neck, gazing down at her as he stepped close. "I love you, Amber."

The smile tugged at the corners of her mouth. "Yeah, me too."

"Really? That's as good as it gets?"

She grinned. "Yep. Now hurry up and kiss me then take me to Ronan's so I can go back to yelling at my grandparents." He obeyed the first part of her demands and when he finally drew away from her, she stared up at him. "I do love you, Kade. And I'm not going to let them kill you."

"You want to tell me why you won't let them kill me? And I know it isn't just because you love me."

She laughed, knowing exactly what he was asking. "You're mine." Her laughter was cut off by another kiss and this time when he drew away slightly, he took her back to Ronan's, through the Void, arriving just outside the room. She stepped inside.

The room was in chaos. Her grandparents were yelling at each other and Ronan was leaning against the wall near the door, asking if they wanted a knife each so they could sort their argument out quicker.

Amber came further into the room. "Enough."

Both her grandparents turned to face her. It was Charles who spoke first. "She sounds exactly like you, Hel."

"Nothing like me," Helen argued.

At the same time, Amber said, "I do not."

Ronan laughed. "And here I was thinking she took after both of you. Most possessive, bloodthirsty, argumentative, contrary human I've come across in ages. A pity she has moments of remorse and wanting to save everyone."

"I'm not bloodthirsty," Amber muttered.

"I'm sure I could think of at least one dragon who'd

agree with me." Ronan strode forward to stop at her side, smiling his predatory smile. "Oh, that's right, she can't anymore, can she?"

"You've killed a dragon?" Helen asked.

Amber nodded.

"How?" Charles demanded.

"What does it matter? She's dead."

"How?" Charles persisted.

"With a sword."

Charles and Helen both beamed at her, sharing a congratulatory look before they turned their smiles back on her.

Amber fought the urge to take a step backwards. "Right. Now we're all talking, what am I going to do with you?"

"Have you still got the sword?" Charles asked.

"Yeah. Now about–"

"Where is it?" Charles asked.

Amber's annoyance increased. "My ahh… bodyguard has it." She'd nearly called him her first warrior, but guessed that would set them off again.

"Your what?" Helen asked.

"Her first warrior," Ronan said.

Amber wanted to hit him. Did he enjoy making trouble?

"Traitor," Helen snarled.

At the same time, Charles growled, "Dragon."

"She's neither Knight nor dragon," Ronan said. "Stop trying to bring her around to your way of thinking. I'm afraid she's far too stubborn to give up her own beliefs."

"What are they?" Charles demanded.

"You don't touch hers. She'll protect them to the death. She doesn't believe in running, but facing all threats head on. And she never gives up," Ronan said.

Amber shook her head. Surely he was exaggerating. She was nothing like that. She only did what she had to.

"She would make a perfect Knight," Charles said.

"She'd make a perfect dragon," Ronan pointed out.

"She is standing right here and is perfectly happy being exactly who she is." Amber glared at each of them, ignoring Kade's chuckle. "All we're figuring out right now is what to do with you." She pointed at her grandparents. "We're wasting time with all this rubbish." Not to mention making her feel highly uncomfortable.

"Set us free and we'll give your dragon time to leave town before we tell the Knights about him," Helen said. "And I won't tell Donna you had me chained up along with your own grandfather."

"If I have to leave town, I fail my test," Kade told Amber.

Even though he'd told her before, she couldn't help hoping for a different answer. *"When does your test finish?"*

"Last day of the year."

"I can't keep them imprisoned that long," Amber burst out.

"What is he telling you?" Charles and Helen demanded at the same time.

She ignored their question. "Your suggestion isn't acceptable."

"See," Ronan said. "You should have listened to me. You don't threaten one of hers."

"He's a dragon," Helen said. "How can you even think of siding with him over your own kind?"

Amber was fed up with them constantly complaining about Kade. "Maybe it runs in the blood. I hear Uncle Roger likes dragons too." At her grandmother's expression, she cursed Ronan for pointing out her tendency for remorse. Raising her chin, she refused to take back her words. They never took theirs back. She forced herself to continue. "I wonder what my cousins are like." She sent a quick look towards Kade. "We should meet them someday."

Kade stepped up beside her, sliding an arm around her waist. "Maybe next time we're at our castle." He momentarily tightened his arm around her.

Amber nodded. "Yeah, next time we're at Temolae Keep."

Charles stilled. "Who did you kill?"

"What is it?" Helen asked her husband.

"Well?" Charles demanded when Amber didn't speak.

Amber was about to answer when she felt two dragons appear in the hallway. She turned to see Alsandair wink at her, before he disappeared into the Void, leaving Rian standing there, her sword in his hand. Kade tensed. She needed to have a talk to Alsandair before Kade decided to kill him after all.

Rian strode forward, bowing and holding out her sword, resting it on both hands. "My lady."

"Don't you dare screw this up, kitten."

Amber sent a quick look towards Ronan, but his face was expressionless. Whatever plan he was hatching he wasn't about to share it with her. If he was going to keep the plan to himself, it'd be his own fault if it got screwed up. She took the sword from Rian and holding it at her side, the point resting on the floor, faced her grandparents again.

"Is that the sword?" Charles asked.

Amber nodded.

"Who did you kill," Charles asked again.

"Paili."

Helen gasped and Charles repeated the name.

"Impossible," Charles said.

"Hold it up and set it alight," Ronan ordered Amber.

She had no idea how that would help, but so far she'd only made progress when Ronan was helping. Although he'd also caused her some setbacks too. Holding the sword up, she widened her stance, pulling away from Kade as her sword blade burst into flame. "I cut her heart nearly in two." She shied away from the thought that Ronan had cut the heart into twenty even pieces, eating a section after having first offered it to her.

"She was in the book," Helen said. "One of the few dragons in there we had a name for."

"My captors spoke of her in tones of fear." Charles' gaze was fixed on the blade.

"What is the point of this?" Amber asked Ronan, her arms starting to ache from holding the sword up for so long.

"They help you till the end of the year. We have Dragon Mages to kill and dragons to hunt. They get to kill as long as they stay away from the Knights," Ronan said.

Amber extinguished the blade, handing it to Rian.

"You don't care what dragons you kill, do you? You just want to kill them."

"No dragon deserves to live." Charles looked at each of the three dragons in the room.

"Then what if I give you the opportunity to hunt dragons. You remain our allies until the last day of the year and then we let you return to your Knights," Amber said.

"We'll be free to hunt who we wish after that," Charles said.

Amber nodded.

"What is the catch?" Charles asked.

"There's no catch," Ronan said. "Maybe we think you'll enjoy working with us so much you won't stop."

"Not likely, dragon," Charles said.

"What else would it involve?" Helen asked.

"You stay in my home, I'll give you access to an area that will be locked off from the main part of the house and you'll help sort through all the information gathered, looking for anything to help us track down the dragons we're trying to find."

"That all seems very one sided. We would be helping remove some of your enemies," Charles said.

"They're dragons. What more do you want?" Ronan asked.

"We'll think on it," Charles said.

"What is there to think about," Amber demanded. "Do you want to kill dragons or not?"

"We want to kill dragons, but we don't want to be told which ones we can and can't kill," Charles said.

"The offer isn't going to last forever." Amber felt like shaking them. Was there nothing they wouldn't argue? "Think of it as earning your freedom. Your ransom wasn't cheap." She couldn't help wondering if Topaz was safe. Were the mages somehow connected to Blair and Irvin? They better not be.

"There must be something else you want. I know I'm not worth a Gold female," Charles said.

"I didn't want your death on my conscience. When they found out you were my grandfather, they'd try and hold me hostage with you."

"I would have killed you before I let that happen," Ronan said to Charles.

"What are you to our granddaughter?" Helen asked.

"Why, we're allies." Ronan turned to Amber, his predatory smile momentarily appearing. "Aren't we, kitten?"

Amber nodded.

"We will expect an answer by Friday." Ronan headed for the door, holding it open. *"Time to go,"* he said to Amber, Kade and Rian. They all filed out of the room, stopping in the hallway while he locked the door. "I'll let you know when they make a decision."

"What do I tell my mum? She'll want to visit them," Amber said.

"Gary can deal with her." Ronan strode away.

Amber stared after him. He could be so annoying sometimes.

"Do you need me or will I return to our lands?" Rian asked.

"No, I'm right." At least she hoped she was. It wasn't like Rian could face her mother for her. "Thanks for bringing my sword."

Rian nodded and strode off in the direction Ronan had taken.

"Where to?" Kade reached for her, holding her close.

"Your place. I guess."

"Straight to my room?"

She hesitated. "No. I probably should get the lecture out of the way."

Kade chuckled, taking them to his front door through the Void.

Chapter Fourteen

All Thursday Amber waited to hear from Ronan while she, Donna and Gary continued to stay at Kade's. It wasn't until Friday evening that Alsandair appeared from the Void as she stepped out of the bathroom, having just finished filling the last of her jewellery with power. A quick mental search showed her Kade was in the lounge room with Brann.

Grabbing hold of Alsandair's forearm, she tugged him outside before he had a chance to speak. Letting him go, she pointed a finger at him. "You stir Kade like that again and I'll tell him I don't care if he kills you. What did you think you were doing winking at me like that?"

"Give me a call when you get bored with Kade and–"

"Stop right there. I'm not interested."

"You kept him from killing me."

She shook her head, barely able to believe what she was hearing. "Are you serious? Did you really think I'd have let him kill you over a misunderstanding? You dragons are unbelievable. I did not save you because I'm interested in you. I saved you because I don't believe in killing people because of a moment of stupidity."

"You think I'm stupid?"

"No," she growled the word. "Why are you here anyway?"

"Ronan sent me."

"Why does he keep sending you? Why not one of his other Golds?"

Alsandair shrugged.

Amber stared at him a moment longer, trying to figure it out. Giving up, she asked, "What's the message?"

"Your grandparents are ready to talk. Ronan wants to see both of you."

She nodded. "Let him know we'll be there soon."

With a nod, Alsandair disappeared into the Void.

Amber sighed heavily, hoping she'd sorted Alsandair out. She'd hate to see him killed over a misunderstanding. Although she was beginning to wonder if it had been more about a dragon seizing what he thought was an opportunity to get close to a mage.

"Amber?" Kade stepped outside. "What are you doing out here?"

"Ronan wants to see us. My grandparents are ready to talk."

"Who brought the message?"

She wanted to tell him that it didn't matter, but she could see it clearly did. "Alsandair."

"Why did you bring him out here?"

"So I could tell him that if he keeps stirring you I won't care if you kill him. Happy?"

"Yeah." Kade stepped forward, a grin in place as he held her. "Is that a promise?"

"It doesn't count if you," she jabbed a finger against his chest, "stir him first."

"Are you ready to go?"

"I need to tell Mum-"

"Brann can tell her." He took them through the Void to Ronan's place before she could object.

"Kade!"

"We didn't have time for a lecture."

"Well you better make time for this one."

They both turned to face Ronan.

"A lecture about what?" Amber asked.

"He's the reason we were attacked at Feralenzi."

Ronan's gaze remained on Amber, but he nodded towards Kade.

"I told no one," Kade said.

Ronan finally looked at Kade. "Except for putting in a request to make it another test. Negotiating for and gaining something of value. Well you nearly lost something of even more value."

"You turned it into a test?" Amber demanded.

Kade nodded.

"What about Flinn? He needs to do tests too." She couldn't help worrying about Crystal, whose fate was currently tied to Flinn's.

"He completed a test last week. Stole something valuable."

"Why didn't Crystal tell me? We talk nearly every day."

"He let her think it was another training exercise."

"He lied to her?" Her anger flared when Kade nodded. "Do you lie to me?"

Kade grinned. "No, but you're more dangerous than Crystal."

Ronan chuckled. "You can't argue that, kitten."

"So what does this mean? No more tests until we catch the other mages?" Amber asked.

"No, it means you need to set up your next test as soon as possible," Ronan said.

Amber stared at Ronan, uncertain if she'd heard right. "You want them to attack us?"

"Bait," Kade said.

"Yes. Draw them out. Let them think we don't know they've got a spy. When they're found, it'll be death. No one can interfere with tests, particularly by sharing information gained from test requests," Ronan said.

"What test?" Amber asked.

Ronan shrugged. "I'm sure Kade can figure one out. It doesn't matter what, just that we bait the trap."

"And Flinn is included. I don't want him and Crystal falling behind." Amber looked at Kade who nodded in answer.

"Flinn will be included because I want all three of you mages there. And when we find Shannon, she will learn what happens to those who cross me." Ronan turned his attention to Kade. "Let me know the details as soon as you figure them out. Make sure it's one where you can have three Golds. I'll play warrior to one of my Golds." He started for the doorway. "Time to see what our reluctant guests have to say."

Amber stared after Ronan, mentally trying to catch up with everything that was happening. It was a wonder any dragon survived more than a handful of years.

"Amber?"

She met Kade's gaze, reaching for his hand. "Yeah, I know. We can't stand here all day." Heading in the direction Ronan had taken, they caught up with him as he was unlocking the door. He checked the room before he let them in.

Charles and Helen rose to their feet the moment Amber stepped into the room. It was Charles who spoke. "We want to talk to our granddaughter alone."

She felt like pointing out that they only claimed her as their granddaughter when it suited them, but guessed starting an argument probably wasn't the best of plans.

"Amber? Do you want to be alone with them?" Ronan directly asked Amber.

She started to say no, then nodded. Her hand tightened on Kade's before she slowly pulled away from him. "I won't be long." When Kade and Ronan left the room, closing the door behind them, she turned back to her grandparents. "What do you want?"

"How well can you control your dragons?" Charles asked.

"I don't own them." She pushed away the memory

of telling Kade he was hers. "They're my allies. Well, Kade is obviously more than that."

"Can you make sure they keep their word?" Helen asked.

"Dragons always keep their word," Amber said.

"They always twist it so they don't have to keep the same word you think you're getting them to keep," Helen said.

She tried not to think about how Ronan had promised to consume only one more dragon heart. Finding out he could do that one-twentieth at a time and practically live forever had not been what they'd expected. "Ronan said you'd be free at the end of the year."

"Death is also freedom." Charles moved as close to her as his chain would allow him. "How do we know it isn't death he's offering us?"

"How do you know it won't be death going up against some dragons?"

"Death in battle is honourable. Death from being tricked by a dragon isn't," Charles said.

"They won't kill you at the end. If you survive to that point, you'll be leaving alive. I'll make sure Ronan says exactly that," Amber said.

"And Kade? You would let him kill us?" Charles asked.

"No. If you need it, he can make the same promise."

"We've talked about it," Charles said.

"We have conditions of our own," Helen added.

"Then I'll call them in so we can discuss them."

Helen shook her head. "No, only the three of us."

"I won't go against them." She met her grandmother's sharp gaze.

"If we work for your dragons until the end of the year, you work for the Knights for the same amount of time," Charles said.

"No." She didn't even have to think about it. Not after seeing what they thought was a crime.

"Yet you would have us work for our enemies," Charles said.

She should have known he was going to be difficult. "You're earning your freedom."

"No. We're betraying our people," Helen said.

"So you won't do it?" Amber asked.

"That depends on you," Charles said. "What do you have against working for the Knights. You don't seem to have any objection to killing dragons."

"The only dragon I've ever killed was one trying to kill me." An image of Paili attacking her, filled her mind. Forcing herself to focus, she pushed the image away. "I won't work for people who kill every dragon they see regardless of what they've done."

"Yet you'll work for a dragon who is a murderer. He's killed someone from your own family," Helen said hotly.

She didn't know what to say. Telling her grandparents that it was better than letting him kill her family probably wouldn't help the situation. But it was more than that now. He knew how to survive and she wasn't going to let anything happen to her friends and family. And everything she learned about him and what he'd experienced had her wondering how he'd managed not to become as bitter as her grandmother. "I won't work for the Knights. I don't work for Ronan. We're allies. I have a say in what happens."

"Do you?" Charles asked.

"Yes." She met his gaze, refusing to look away. "What's your answer?"

Charles didn't look away either. "That you will at least meet the Knights and give them a chance. You only have the dragons' side of things. Give the Knights six months to prove themselves."

It didn't look like he was going to give in on the subject. "I will give them a month. That's more time than necessary," Amber said.

"You will keep an open mind and not shame us in front of our people," Charles said.

"I won't stand by and let them harm any of my people," Amber warned.

"Dragons aren't people," Helen snarled.

Amber didn't even look at Helen, she continued to hold Charles' gaze. "Well?"

"We'll help you kill dragons, but we won't do anything to harm our people," Charles said.

Amber nodded, holding his gaze a moment longer before she opened the door. *"You can come in,"* she said to Ronan and Kade.

Chapter Fifteen

Amber pushed the shopping trolley while her mother walked beside her. She wondered if it was possible to learn how to not give in to guilt. Ronan would probably tell her it was only a matter of not being so weak. But he hadn't been there last night when her mother had begged her to take her to her parents and then complained how there was nothing normal about their lives anymore. If spending a Saturday morning doing grocery shopping was the highlight of a normal life, maybe her crazy one wasn't so bad.

Donna reached for a bottle of herbs, dropping them into the half full trolley. "We haven't done this in ages." She smiled at Amber as they turned into the next aisle.

"Maybe because I hate going grocery shopping."

"At least no one is trying to kill you here," Donna said.

The lady ahead of them stopped suddenly and Amber nearly ran into her. "Great."

"Wait up." Donna stopped in front of a shelf, trying to reach one of the jars at the top.

"Let me get that for you." A man who had entered the aisle, hurried forward. He handed the jar to Donna and smiled.

"Oh, hello." Donna returned the smile. "I'm afraid I've forgotten your name."

"Wayne Smith." He looked towards Amber. "Is this your daughter?"

"Yes, this is Amber." Donna placed the jar into the trolley. "How is your daughter? Uhm, Jennifer, isn't it?"

Wayne chuckled. "At least you remembered one of us."

"Mum, I've got other plans for the day, remember?" Amber stared at her mother, wishing she could talk directly to her mind so she could remind her that she'd only agreed to two hours. The rest of the day was hers. And she wasn't about to spend it shopping with her mother. This wasn't fun. It was a chore.

Donna ignored her, continuing to chat with Wayne. Amber glared at the man, wondering who he was. He looked a little younger than her mother and was probably a gym junkie if the muscular arms showing beneath the sleeves of his t-shirt were anything to go by. He had sandy brown hair, which was little more than stubble, and a ready smile. Her gaze narrowed. The man smelled odd under his excess of aftershave.

"Mum." Amber couldn't keep the annoyance out of her tone. "Gary will be wondering where we are."

"Gary?" Wayne looked from Donna to Amber.

"A friend of mine," Donna said.

"Her boyfriend," Amber added.

"Well, I'll let you go then, but my offer for dinner is still open. My daughter and I know very few people here. It's tough being new to a town. It'd be nice for her to meet someone her own age. And you're welcome to bring your boyfriend along too." Wayne's smile never slipped.

"No teenager wants their parents choosing friends for them. I'm sure she'll meet enough kids at school." The last thing Amber wanted was her mother organising her social life. If her mother thought grocery shopping was fun then she hated to think what she'd arrange for her social life.

"She's homeschooled and there isn't much in this area for homeschooled kids." Wayne reached for Donna's hand. "It was lovely to run into you again."

With another smile in Amber's direction, he wheeled his empty trolley down the aisle.

"Where do you know him from?" Amber asked.

"I've run into him a few times. He's a lovely man. Lost his wife a few years ago."

"What about Gary."

"Oh, it's nothing like that. Wayne wouldn't be interested in me. He's about six years younger than me." Donna started walking along the aisle.

"Good. I don't like the way he smells." Amber pushed the trolley, looking ahead to Wayne who was turning at the end of the aisle.

"Amber! Hush." Donna glanced behind them. "Don't talk about people like that."

"Let's just get this over with." They turned into the next aisle and Amber was relieved Wayne wasn't in sight. It was bad enough shopping with her mother without having to talk to some old guy whose daughter needed friends. The last thing she wanted in her life was more people to worry about.

By the time they returned to Kade's place, Amber was barely holding onto her temper. The car drive home had been spent arguing with her mother. When they pulled up, Amber flung the door open, half out of the car before she turned back to her mother. "Don't you understand? My life will never be normal. Ever." She slammed the door behind her, striding towards the house.

Brann came out before she reached it, passing her with a nod, headed for her mother's car. She stopped a moment to see what he was doing, turning away when he started gathering grocery bags.

Kade stood in the doorway, watching her, a hand on the door frame. *"Do you want to go hunting?"*

The panther stirred, but she shook her head.

Kade pushed away from the door frame, slowly crossing the distance between them. He stopped in front of her. "You can't avoid it. Hunting helps calm the wild animal."

"All I'm interested in is what you're doing about your next test."

"Flinn and I were talking about doing it next weekend. Think your mum will tell Crystal's mum she's staying with you?"

Amber groaned. "She's more likely to tell Crystal's mum what's going on."

"Flinn's trying to convince Crystal to move in with him."

The last thing she wanted was Crystal completely dependent on Flinn. She bet her mother would feel the same way, although not for the same reasons. "I'll see what I can do." She looked towards her mother disappearing into the house with some groceries, Brann following with the rest. Another argument was the last thing she wanted. She felt the panther stir. "Maybe we should go hunting."

Kade grinned. "Want a lift or you flying yourself?"

She didn't bother answering him. Since she was dressed in dragon-leather, she forced the panther away, changing into a goshawk and taking to the air. *"Try and keep up."* She felt Kade's amusement as he took to the air behind her.

Diving into the scrub behind the house, she flushed some smaller birds from the long grass. Instinct had her swooping after them, but she veered off. She was more than an animal. Far overhead, she could sense Kade, staying well above view in case anyone was about. She mentally searched, finding only animals in this direction.

"It's safe. No one for miles."

Kade flew down in front of her. Diving towards the ground and then pulling up again as a wallaby jumped from the trees to bound across open ground.

Again Amber reined in the instinct to give chase. Sometimes the panther wanted to go after creatures far too big for the goshawk. Ahead and to her left was a pigeon and she changed direction slightly. The distance between them narrowed, her concentration focused on her prey.

Above her a dragon flashed in and out of the Void, breaking her focus. Amber angled upwards, trying to recall everything she'd sensed about the dragon. There was nothing she recognised. *"Kade? Did you see it? Another Gold."*

"No. Where was it?"

"Above us, but it's gone now."

"Maybe we should return home."

"I want to call Ronan. See if he's got someone watching me." Amber flew towards the ground, mentally searching the area before she landed and changed into human form.

Kade landed beside her, changing, a hand reaching for her waist to tug her closer. "If you notice them again, tell me and I'll get us straight out of here."

"What if they were friendly? That's possible, isn't it?"

"Yeah."

She eyed him, not sure if she heard a touch of scepticism in his tone. "So I could be paranoid about nothing."

"It's the paranoid dragons that live the longest."

His words made her think about Ronan and his belief that friends were enemies that hadn't got around to stabbing you in the back yet. "I'll call Ronan." Taking her phone from her pocket, she once again tried not to think about where it went when she became an animal. Were some of her animal parts made of electronics when she changed? Nope, she wasn't going to think about it. Instead, she dialled Ronan's number.

"They're still alive."

"I wasn't ringing about my grandparents. Do you have any Golds watching me?" Again she searched the area.

"No. You sent him back, remember?"

For once she wished he'd ignored her. "Okay. See you." She mentally searched the area again.

"Don't you dare hang up. What's this about?"

"I noticed a Gold flash in and out of the Void way behind Kade's place while we were out hunting." Again she checked the area. They were still alone.

"A young one?"

"What?"

"Young Golds can't stay in the Void for long periods of time. They flash in and out. When they first start some of them can only manage ten minutes. Was it a young dragon?"

"I don't know."

"Does Kade?"

"He didn't notice them."

"Male or female?"

She felt like growling at all the questions he fired at her. "It was so quick I barely realised they were there. Only that they didn't seem familiar."

"I'll send Chait to watch you."

She shouldn't have rung him. "I don't need a bodyguard."

"With all the time I've invested in you, I'm not about to let some stray dragon kill you. Now go home and wait for Chait. If you're not there shortly your grandparents won't get fed today." Ronan disconnected.

"Damn dragon." Amber glared at the phone.

"You want me to take you home?"

She bit back her first instinct, which was to refuse, then decided it wouldn't help her grandparents trust dragons if she let them starve. "Yeah. I suppose."

"We can hunt once we collect Chait."

Amber opened her mouth to tell him it was rude to listen in on other people's conversations, then closed it. Why bother when he'd keep doing it anyway. "Fine."

Kade grinned. "You'll feel better once you've hunted."

"So you keep telling me," she muttered. She had a

feeling it was going to take a lot more than hunting to make her feel better. Especially at the rate her problems were piling up in her life.

Chapter Sixteen

Amber paced the lounge room floor, ignoring the looks her mother kept sending her. It had taken hours to convince her last week that keeping Crystal's secret was better than having her leave home at sixteen. She mentally searched the skies again. Couldn't Flinn and his warriors fly any faster? If he'd been less stubborn about not relying on others, Ronan would have sent Golds to take him through the Void. She'd waited all week to see Crystal and they only had tonight before the rest of the weekend was given over to the next test. She didn't want them to waste a single moment. Enough time had been wasted at school today. Maybe Crystal was right and school was a waste of time for Dragon Mages. No, she couldn't think like that. She wasn't about to give up all her plans for her life. This year finish year twelve, next year uni.

Out the front, four dragons popped out of the

Void, two disappearing back into it. Amber ran for the front door, flinging it open with a smile. "Maira. What are you doing here?"

Maira hurried forward, throwing her arms around Amber, chunky silver and black bracelets glinting in the afternoon light. "I'm back for good, Rian temporarily." She drew away from Amber, looking past her.

Amber let her go when she sensed Brann behind her. She turned to Rian. "How temporarily?"

"I leave Monday. I need to keep an eye on the new dragons for a while to make sure they know what they are doing," Rian said.

Before Amber could say anything else, Flinn and his warriors landed in dragon form and she watched as Crystal clambered out of the dragon saddle and ran towards her. "I thought you'd never get here."

Crystal hugged Amber tightly. "We had to go in a million different directions. I couldn't see a single Gold hiding in the Void, but would he listen?" She sent a glare in Flinn's direction. "Of course not. He said it pays not to be complacent. I think he just wanted to drive me crazy."

"That wouldn't surprise me." Amber drew back, grabbing Crystal's hand. "Come on. It's your turn to get a lecture from my mum."

Crystal rolled her eyes. "I seriously can't believe you told her about me."

"She wasn't going to let you stay here otherwise. Reckoned it was too dangerous."

Crystal laughed as Amber opened the front door. *"Better not tell her about any of our battles then."*

"I'm not crazy." She paused as she saw her mother's expression. "Well, not yet."

"Crystal. Have you got a moment?" Donna asked.

"Sure." Crystal exchanged a look with Amber. *"It's not like I really have a choice."*

"Not at all." Amber let go of Crystal's hand.

"In the kitchen, please." Donna led the way.

"Can you come and rescue me if it goes on for too long?" Crystal asked.

"I'll send Rian. He's probably the most diplomatic out of all of us," Amber said.

Crystal giggled. "Yeah, with you and Flinn being the least." She strode towards the doorway, throwing over her shoulder. "Fifteen minutes, right?"

"Sure." Amber watched Crystal leave the room, annoyed that even more of their time was about to be wasted. But she guessed she couldn't complain too much. Her mother had got Crystal here and that was good. Or she hoped it was.

In the end, Amber didn't need to send Rian to

rescue Crystal. She returned to the lounge room thirteen minutes later and the two of them threw on a movie and ignored it as they spent the rest of the night catching up on news.

When they both headed to bed, Crystal to Flinn's room and Amber to Kade's, Donna cornered Amber in the hallway. "What do I tell Crystal's mum if something happens to her while she's here?"

"You won't have to tell her anything. That will be someone else's job."

"Someone who'll cover up what really happens?"

Amber nodded.

"And what if something happens to you? Will I hear the truth about that?"

"Yeah. They won't have to hide the truth from you since you already know."

"Don't go, Amber."

"I have to. And anyway, it's not that big a deal. We'll be back by Sunday afternoon at the latest."

"I'm not an idiot. I've heard bits and pieces all week. You're planning to fight. And not in some stupid schoolyard scrape. A full on life or death battle."

"Mum, I'll be okay."

"Like my father was? Like my brother? Neither

of them came home and they weren't even facing battle."

Guilt hit her at the worry in her mother's eyes. "It's not my first battle."

"Is that meant to make me feel any better?"

"Uhm, maybe?"

"It doesn't. You're a child. Barely seventeen. This wasn't what I wanted for you. For either of you. How could you let your brother be caught up in this?"

Guilt was instantly replaced by anger. "In case you haven't noticed, Jay is older than me. He makes his own choices and lives his own life. It wasn't like I held a knife at his throat and forced him to become a mage."

"I could lose both of you tomorrow."

Amber didn't know what to say. Her anger faded a little.

"And I haven't even had a chance to say goodbye to Jasper."

"He'll be here in the morning."

"For a handful of minutes."

"What do you want me to say? That I'm sorry? I'll be the one out there fighting for my life, not you. I–" she broke off, not wanting to get into an argument. "I need to get some sleep." She started towards Kade's door.

"Amber?"

She stopped, staring straight ahead. The door handle was shiny, far newer than the timber door. "What?"

"Take care tomorrow."

"Okay."

"Wake me before you go?"

Amber looked over her shoulder. The silence stretched between them until she answered. "Okay." She continued to Kade's room, letting herself inside to lean against the door.

Kade came forward to take her hand, drawing her to the bed. "Are you okay?"

She thought about his question. "I wouldn't have a clue." Dropping onto the bed, she sighed heavily. "What was I meant to have said to her?"

"I don't know. Humans are far different from dragons. Kiani would have told me to remember all I've been taught and not to shame the clan by failing."

She wasn't sure which mother she preferred. Maybe one somewhere in between. "And if you died?"

Kade shifted Amber to her side of the bed so he could lie down. "She would be thankful that she'd chosen to have more than one child."

"Would she be sad?"

"Disappointment would be the greater emotion. She'd be disappointed that I'd failed the clan and hadn't proven to be the fittest."

Amber fell silent, not knowing what she could say to that. And yet Kade didn't sound at all bothered by his mother's attitude. Sometimes she couldn't understand dragons. She fell asleep thinking of all the things about dragons that didn't make sense, waking to the beep of the alarm on her phone. Turning it off, she lay there for a moment mentally checking where everyone was in the house.

Flinn and Crystal were still in his room, along with his warriors who were near his door since Donna and Gary had taken over their room. Gary was in his room, alone. She searched more of the house until she found her mother in the kitchen, Jasper with her.

Amber climbed out of bed, grabbing her jacket from the floor. "Jay's here." She stopped at the door. "And he's talking to Mum in the kitchen."

Kade, who'd been in the process of rising from the bed, sat back on the edge. "I'll let you have some time with your family before we leave."

"Coward."

Kade grinned. "I don't see you rushing out there."

Amber sighed. "I'm going." Her tone sounded as enthusiastic as she felt. It took her a few more seconds before she could bring herself to open the door and step into the hallway.

When she reached the kitchen, Jasper stood with an arm around Donna who was seated at the table, her head in her hands, crying. Amber nearly turned and headed back to the bedroom, but Jasper looked in her direction.

"Don't even think of bailing," he thought directly to her. "Mum, Amber's here. Why don't I make something for all of us to eat?"

Rian came into the kitchen. "I will make breakfast. The lounge room is empty."

"Come on, Mum." Jasper sent Amber a daggered look. *"Maybe you better teach your warrior when not to interfere."*

Amber grinned. *"He was looking out for me, not you."* She followed Jasper and Donna to the lounge room. "Mum, we'll be back Sunday."

"You can't guarantee that," Donna said.

Jasper started to speak, but Amber interrupted. "There are no guarantees." She met her mother's gaze. "Ever."

"I don't expect guarantees. I just don't want the two of you to go running headlong into danger," Donna said. "Being part of this dragon world doesn't mean you have to chase danger."

Ronan stepped out of the Void. "They will return. Keeping my mages alive is my current priority."

"You don't own us," Amber said.

"Are you saying you're not mine?"

Amber started to agree, then stopped. What was Ronan up to now? "No one owns us, but you are responsible for keeping us alive." She could have sworn that for a split second a look of approval crossed his face.

Ronan nodded. "You may learn yet." His gaze travelled around the lounge room. "In the kitchen. We'll do the last of our planning over breakfast."

Amber started to follow Ronan and Jasper, but her mother put a hand on her shoulder. "What?" She was unsuccessful at keeping the impatience from her voice.

"Will he keep you safe? My mother told me all sorts of stories about dragons. They all boiled down to not being able to trust them."

"Dragons always keep their word. He wasn't lying when he said keeping us alive is his current priority. He needs what we can do."

"And what happens when he no longer needs you?"

"We won't be his priority." Annoyance hit Amber

at the expression that filled her mother's face. "You told me to stop lying to you."

"I didn't say anything."

"No, you just looked like you were about to faint or something." Amber glanced towards the doorway leading to the hallway. "I need to join the planning discussion. Otherwise, I won't know what's going on." Without waiting for an answer, she strode to the kitchen, leaving her mother behind.

Joining the crowd at the table, she squeezed in beside Kade. Over a cooked breakfast, Ronan explained the plan. Once they'd eaten, and Rian cleared the table, he rolled out a map so they could see where all the local allies were for the clan they were attacking. She began to wonder if the most difficult clan had been chosen to attack. What if they called on their allies to help? They certainly had enough of them nearby.

Rising to his feet and rolling up the map, Ronan said, "Even though this is a test, raiding an enemy of your clan isn't the main objective. If you need to drop the spoils to get the enemy off your tail when the other mages attack, you drop them. We need to capture one of those mages and take out their dragons. Aim for the wings." Ronan met Amber's gaze. "They won't have any qualms about aiming for ours."

When everyone rose from the table, Donna hurried forward, grabbing first Amber's hand and then Jasper's, pulling them to the side. "You make sure you look out for each other." She pulled them in close, hugging both of them.

Amber tried to draw away. "Mum. We have to go."

Donna released her. "Let me know when you're safe. As soon as the battle is over."

"Our phones work in their lands," Jasper said. "You could ring us tomorrow if you want."

"I still expect you to call me the moment it's over."

"It's more than just the battle. We'll call as soon as we get the chance," Amber said.

Donna dragged them in for another hug. "Be careful."

"Okay." Amber pulled away again. "Gee, why not tell us to wear clean underwear too."

Ronan and his gold dragon joined them. "Jasper, you'll ride Turi. He hasn't passed all his tests yet so he seemed the logical choice."

Jasper nodded before he turned back to Donna. "See you, Mum." She dragged him in for another hug before he unwrapped her arms from around him and, with a grin and a wave, clasped Turi's forearm and nodded to the dragon. They disappeared into the Void.

"Is that safe?" Donna asked.

"Safer than crossing the road. Look, Mum, I have to go. I'll call you, right?"

Donna nodded and Amber stepped back when it looked like her mother would hug her again. Feeling Kade behind her, she turned her head towards him. *"Get me out of here now."* Kade wrapped his arms around her and took her through the Void to the gathering point.

Rian came forward with a dragon saddle and put it on Kade as soon as he changed forms. During the next few minutes everyone prepared, taking to the air once they were ready.

"You all know your directions," Ronan told everyone. *"Move out."*

Amber watched as Flinn flew towards the left, Crystal on his back, his warriors on each side of him. Turi, Jasper on his back with Ronan and Brann flanking him, headed for the right. Kade gave them some time before he flew straight ahead, Maira and Rian flying with him. Amber mentally searched ahead, looking for trouble. Unlike Crystal, she wouldn't be able to find trouble if it was hiding in the Void.

When they were within sight of the castle, Amber released herself from the saddle, turning into a goshawk as she let go. Fear and uncertainty evaporated as animal instinct kicked in and her first thought was to chase the birds in the distance. She forced that urge away and flew towards the castle, coming at it from a different angle to the dragons.

Ahead she could sense Crystal and Jasper, also in goshawk form. So far everything was going according to plan, even to the dragons pouring out of the castle and headed for Kade, Maira and Rian. Mentally searching she found the other two teams already in battle. The one thing she didn't find were any humans. She had no idea what they'd do if they failed to lure out the Dragon Mages. She guessed Ronan would make them organise yet another test to complete.

Drawing her wings in close, Amber flew in through one of the upper windows, landing on the floor and turning human when she found the bedroom empty. Now to locate the treasure she was after. She opened the door slightly, listening and mentally searching. The corridor was empty. Racing along it, she continued searching her surroundings, hoping no one was hiding in the Void. Reaching the end of the corridor, she headed up the stairs, following the directions Ronan had given her earlier. It was taking her longer than she'd expected. The castle was much bigger than it had looked on paper.

"Are you okay?" she asked Kade, finally reaching the top of the stairs and coming out into a tower room with barred windows.

"Just hurry up."

That hadn't been the answer she was looking for. Spying the wooden chest sitting under one of the windows, she crossed the small room and tried to open it. The lid didn't budge. It was locked like Ronan had said it would be.

Grabbing a handle, she tugged it towards the stairs, pushing it down them. The chest crashed against the stone wall, but stayed intact. Wincing at the noise, Amber ran down the stairs to push it down the next flight, swearing when it still didn't break. Drawing on the strength of her panther, she hoisted the chest onto the stair rails, balancing it as she peered down the stairwell. Three stories. If that didn't break it she had no idea what to do. Giving it a shove, she held her breath, letting it out in a rush as the chest smashed onto the floor below. Turning into a goshawk, she flew down the stairwell, dodging to the side when four warriors ran towards her, attacking with swords.

Chapter Seventeen

Amber circled around, darting in when one of the warriors tried to pick up a drawstring bag from the shattered remains of the chest. Grabbing the strings, she flew towards the nearest window, ignoring the shouts behind her. *"Got it."* She sent the message to all those with her.

"There's four Golds hiding in the Void. I can't get to my location," Crystal said.

"I'll have my target in a minute. Someone better be ready to grab the sword when I throw it out the window," Jasper warned.

"Crystal, get out of there. Jasper, hurry up. I'm still waiting. Amber, retreat with your team," Ronan ordered.

"But I don't want to be the only one who fails," Crystal protested. *"What if we end up completely failing?"*

"As long as we capture a mage, only one treasure needs

to be brought back for all of us to pass the test. I didn't want it riding on one item," Flinn said. *"Now get out of there and don't take stupid risks."*

"Okay."

Amber was relieved to hear Crystal agree to retreat. Behind her was the sound of wings. Not having time to look, she mentally searched and found the four dragons who'd attacked her. They weren't far behind. Searching ahead she found her team battling nine dragons. The odds didn't look good. The dragons behind her came closer since she was unable to fly as fast as usual carrying the bag. But she couldn't drop it. She knew Crystal would be tempted to go back for her treasure if she did.

"Ready Ronan? I'm throwing the sword out," Jasper said.

"Now," Ronan said.

"What's taking you so long, Amber?" Kade demanded.

"The treasure is slowing me down."

"Ditch it," Kade said.

"No," Flinn said. *"That'll only give us one treasure. It's too early to be down to a single treasure."*

Amber hated to agree with Flinn, but he was right. It was too soon to be down to one treasure.

"So it's okay for my mage to take risks, but not yours?" Kade demanded.

"Everyone get out of here. Rian, do your job and help Amber," Ronan ordered.

"Where are you?" Rian asked Amber.

"Straight ahead. You should see me soon." She spoke to Rian alone, tracking him as he came closer. Several dragons followed him.

"When I am close enough, drop the bag and I will catch it. Then get out of here," Rian said.

Amber waited until he was nearly upon her before she let go of the bag, wheeling back towards the dragons that were chasing her, dodging between them.

"What are you doing? Get out of here," Rian said.

Amber screeched angrily when she realised he'd broadcast his question to their entire team.

"What are you doing, Amber? Follow orders and retreat," Ronan said.

"We'll never make it." She dodged dragon flames. *"You get out of here, Rian. That's an order."*

"What are you planning?" Jasper asked.

She checked where her brother was, finding him rapidly drawing near. *"I think we can take one. Make it crazy."* She sent the words to her brother only.

"*You better not get yourself killed,*" Ronan said directly to Amber. "*The rest are fair game if you're dead.*"

"*I know.*" Seeing her brother come close, she dropped onto one of the dragons, turning human. Clinging to his back, she forced several fireballs into him, Jasper doing the same. When the dragon spun in midair, roaring, she was thrown from his back. As she turned into a goshawk, she checked his mind, finding nothing sane. She screeched a victory cry as the dragon turned on his companions and the other two stopped to help. Now for the ones who'd continued to chase Rian.

Jasper flew beside her. "*Are you trying to get us killed? Mum would have a heart attack if she knew we'd done that.*"

"*It worked, didn't it? And I didn't hear you argue before we did it.*"

"*I didn't expect it to be so dangerous.*"

"*Make yourself useful and deal with the ones chasing me. They're slowing me down,*" Ronan said.

Amber searched for him, finding him not far behind her. "*I thought you were worried I was going to get myself killed.*"

"Don't be smart, kitten. And try and control your smugness. I can feel it from here."

If she could have laughed, she would have at Ronan's comment. Instead, she screeched again, changing direction, Jasper at her side. *"Let's take the one in the middle."*

"I bet I get to him first," Jasper said.

"I doubt it." She dropped down, landing on the dragon to become human, Jasper doing the same. Clinging to the dragon that twisted in midair, Amber forced several fireballs into him before she was flung through the air. It was harder to change this time and panic momentarily rushed through her as the ground came closer. Then she was changing and flying upwards, searching out the dragon her and Jasper had attacked. He was feral, not a single shred of sanity to be found.

"Amber, where are you?" Kade asked.

"Coming." She wheeled around and flew towards Ronan who carried the sword in his claws, Jasper flying with her.

"Well hurry up and stop pulling crazy stunts."

"Rian told you, didn't he?"

"Mages!" Flinn warned.

"Where?" Ronan demanded.

"Coming from my direction," Flinn said.

"Everyone to Flinn," Ronan said.

"Maira and I still have too many dragons attacking us," Kade said.

"Rian ditch your treasure and go help them," Ronan said.

"No!" Flinn and Amber said at the same time.

"Rian you head for the drop point and Jasper and I will help Kade and Maira," Amber said.

"Who is organising this?" Ronan demanded.

"Are you lot trying to get us killed?" Flinn asked.

"I still have dragons chasing me," Rian said.

"Then head to Kade. We'll deal with them." Amber saw Kade and Maira ahead. Jasper continued to fly at her side, but Ronan had circled away to head towards Flinn. *"We'll be there in a minute. It won't take us long to deal with this."* Darting between two dragons, she landed on one and became human, Jasper with her. She forced fireballs into the dragon until she was flung off by his erratic movements.

"Amber!" Kade's mental shout was accompanied by a roar.

Answering him was beyond her, she was too busy trying to change into a goshawk as the ground rapidly approached. Tree branches whipped at her just before she changed shape and darted between the trees, headed for the sky.

"*No more taking chances.*" Kade flew in close.

"*One more.*" She aimed for one of the dragons chasing Rian. "*You up to this?*" She sent the question to her brother.

"*Always.*"

They landed on one of the dragons, forcing fireballs into him. Amber dropped away before the dragon could throw her from him, changing shape and flying towards Kade.

"*I will take the treasure to safety.*" Rian wheeled in the sky, the dragons who'd been chasing him now fighting each other.

Amber landed in the dragon saddle, becoming human and strapping herself in. "*I'm fine.*" She drew power from her bracelets before she healed the cuts on her body, the worst of them on her arms and face. Looking over her shoulder, she saw the dragons her and Jasper had made feral causing plenty of problems for their companions. Checking that Jasper was fine, she was relieved to see him flying nearby.

"*Then why can I smell blood?*"

Her gaze was drawn to the streaks of blood smeared across her arms. "*They were barely scratches. Go help Flinn and Crystal.*"

"*We will talk about this later,*" Kade warned.

"You won't need to. I'm sure Ronan will have more than enough to say. Now hurry up."

"Is anyone else coming? And don't let anyone get that sword Ronan dropped. We can collect it when we've dealt with the mages," Flinn said.

Amber searched the area around Flinn and his team. *"There's four Dragon Mages and eleven dragons."*

"Then why aren't you here already? Do you expect us to deal with them on our own?"

Flinn's words annoyed Amber. *"We're coming. As if I'd leave Crystal behind."*

"You will fight from my back," Kade ordered.

Amber smiled. *"We'll see."* She'd do whatever it took to survive this battle. And make sure her people survived too.

Kade banked sharply. *"We won't see. You'll stay on my back."*

Amber laughed at his movement. It was better than a roller coaster ride. *"Just hurry up. I don't want anything to happen to Crystal."* As they came closer, she called fireballs to her hands, readying them to throw.

Kade dropped sharply as one of the mages threw fire at them and Amber threw her own the moment his flying steadied. Fire, lightning and ice was thrown around and Amber began to worry that they couldn't win. Drawing more power from her bracelets, she released herself from the saddle, ignoring Kade's bellow as she changed form, calling Jasper to help her.

Darting in amongst the dragons, she latched onto one, turning human and forcing fireballs into it, Jasper once again at her side. This time she let go of the dragon before he could fling her from his back and quickly changed into a goshawk, darting away. The dragon roared, attacking those nearest him. Fighting his friends.

"Are you crazy?" Crystal demanded.

"Probably." Amber darted between two more dragons. If it took being crazy to survive then she had no problems with that. *"Ready, Jasper?"*

"I must be crazy too since I'm going along with the idea."

The moment Amber became human, she laughed, forcing fireballs into the dragon, as did her brother. Letting go, she turned into a goshawk, flying out of the way as the dragon snapped at her. When he gave chase, she came in close to one of his friends, relieved when he attacked the other dragon instead of continuing to give chase.

"These mages smell bodd," Maira said.

"In what way?" Amber asked.

"Human and dragon. I can't smell anything else," Maira said.

"Don't let them fall. We need at least one alive," Ronan said.

"How are we meant to do that?" Amber asked.

"Get back in a saddle and throw fire at the wings of the dragons they're riding."

Since there were only the dragons ridden by the mages after them, Amber decided to follow Ronan's order, returning to Kade. *"I don't know how that will help. They'll go down with their dragon."*

"Once their dragon is out of action, I'll fly in and slash at the straps holding the mage in the saddle and Maira can grab the mage," Ronan said.

"There's a gold dragon hiding in the Void," Crystal said. *"And it's not one of the officials. They're a lot further back."*

"What's it doing?" Ronan asked.

"Watching."

"Tell me if that changes."

"Okay," Crystal said.

Amber hoped the dragon didn't mean trouble. They had more than enough to deal with and she was getting tired. She threw another fireball at the wings of one of the dragons, but it was nearly impossible to hit with the way Kade kept dodging the fireballs aimed at him. Looking around she saw that Jasper and Crystal weren't having any better luck.

"This isn't going to work." Drawing more power from her bracelets, she unstrapped herself, becoming a goshawk. *"You better catch the mage, Maira."* She flew straight towards the mage that had been attacking her, darting between fireballs and ice. Then she collided with the mage, turning human as she wrapped an arm around the man, unstrapping him from the saddle. They both fell towards the ground, the man bellowing as Amber became a goshawk and slipped from his arms that had gone around her as they'd fallen.

"Got him," Maira said.

Amber's victory screech was cut off in mid cry as a dragon grabbed her out of mid air.

"Gold coming in fast," Crystal warned.

Amber struggled to get free, Kade and Ronan both flying towards the mageless dragon that had captured her.

"Where?" Ronan demanded.

The gold dragon flashed out of the Void, slashing at the dragon who held Amber, disappearing so quickly that Amber doubted for a moment that it had happened. But the dragon released her, screaming as he turned on his attacker who was already gone. Then Ronan and Kade were on him, tearing at his wings, letting go as he spiralled quickly to the ground. Amber flew upwards, refusing to look or even search in his direction, trying not to think about him colliding with the earth. From this height, he wouldn't survive.

"The gold is going back to watching. Think they're a friend?" Crystal asked.

"What makes you say that?" Flinn asked.

"They attacked the dragon that had caught Amber."

"They better not cause us to lose this test." The anger was clear in Flinn's thoughts.

Amber hoped the Gold had been too quick for the dragons observing their test to have noticed. Although Kade had told her they could have easily had another two Golds join them on this test if they'd been willing to trust any others.

"Are you okay?" Kade flew towards her.

She landed on the saddle and, becoming human, strapped herself in. *"Let's deal with the rest of them."* Her body ached from the crushing grip of the dragon. Seeing how few bracelets had power, she decided not to heal herself for now. She wanted to ask Kade if he'd noticed the gold that had flashed out of the Void to help her, but there was no time. They still had another three dragons and mages to deal with.

"You want to send another one feral?" Jasper asked.

"I'm running low on power." Amber sent her thoughts to Jasper only.

"You've still got some stored. We can't keep dodging the mages all day. One of us will get hurt," Jasper said.

She really wanted to say yes. Instead, she sent a fireball at the mage attacking her and Kade. *"I need some reserves."* Then she sent her thoughts to all her companions. *"Focus on the one. Outnumber him."*

"The one Amber is attacking first, then the female dragon second," Ronan said. *"Try and capture mages if possible. Orin can collect the next one if I get him free from the saddle."*

They all attacked at once, one of the dragon's wings shredded, making him plummet towards the ground. It was too quick for them to capture the mage, but they managed to take the next one, Orin flying away with him. The other dragon and mage disappeared into the Void.

"Cowards," Crystal said. *"They've left the area completely."*

"What about the one that's watching?" Ronan asked.

"Keeping their distance," Crystal said.

Flinn flew towards the ground, scooping up the sword before he aimed skywards. *"Meeting point. Let's get this test wrapped up."* He wheeled, heading in the correct direction.

Chapter Eighteen

Amber wanted to argue, but she really wanted the tests done as soon as possible. Flinn needed to pass them so he could create his own clan. Then Crystal wouldn't be in such a precarious position. Only the strongest survived and the strongest weren't usually clanless.

When they reached the meeting point, they landed in front of the two dragons that were in human form. Orin, Maira and Rian stood near them. Two more dragons joined them, becoming human as they landed beside the officials.

"Are you fine?" Rian asked Amber directly.

She nodded.

"They would not allow us to return to the fight. They said if we did not guard the treasure we would fail the test."

"I'm glad you stayed." Amber turned her attention to Kade, who gestured towards the mages.

"Two treasures taken from enemies and two captives taken from battle." Kade gestured towards the mages.

"These are humans," one of the officials said.

"Dragon Mages," Ronan corrected. "You." He pointed to one of the men. "Prove what you are or die."

The mage formed a ball of ice in his hand, throwing it at the ground. Shards exploded around his feet.

Ronan growled at him, "Don't be smart. You can still die."

"I–"

Ronan cuffed the man across the head and he abruptly ceased speaking.

The official nodded. "We will let you know your results as soon as the assessment is complete."

"We'll let you know if our interrogation gives the name of the ones leaking information about test locations," Ronan said.

"Interrogation? No one said anything about interrogation." The mage who'd called ice tried to pull away from Maira. There was fear in his voice.

No one paid him any attention, other than Maira who tightened her grip on him.

"We are secure. The leak must be your problem," an official said.

"This is the second time. There was no leak on our side," Ronan said.

"Ronan, your Golds are here now, waiting in the Void," Crystal spoke to their entire team.

An official stepped forward. "One of us will need to be there to verify the information gained."

Ronan nodded. "I'll take you to the secure location we've organised." He made a motion with his hand and two Golds stepped out of the Void, taking the mages into the Void with them. Ronan held out a hand to the official.

"Your home?"

"No. A secure location." Ronan smiled.

Amber watched as the official took Ronan's hand and they disappeared. She wished she could do the same. How much longer did they need to stand around here?

Flinn stepped forward, holding out the sword. "One of the treasures for you to verify the value." When the official took it from him, he beckoned Rian forward.

Rian looked at Amber first and she nodded. He

tipped the contents of the drawstring bag into his hand. A diamond necklace slithered out to lay glittering in his palm.

"No wonder the bag was so heavy," Amber muttered. "When you said diamond necklace I thought you meant a pendant on a chain. Not an entire string of diamonds."

Crystal reached out to run a finger across the stones. "It's beautiful."

"You're not keeping it," Flinn growled.

Crystal glared at him. "I wasn't planning to." Her gaze followed the necklace as one of the officials took it. "But it would look awesome on me."

"We will be in touch." The rest of the officials disappeared into the Void.

"It looks like I wasn't the only one who thought the necklace beautiful. That dragon came in for a look and turned into a girl," Crystal said.

"Drag her out of the Void. I'll take her back to our castle," Kade said.

"Stop endangering my mage. The girl could just as easily pull Crystal into the Void," Flinn said.

Crystal pulled a girl from the Void, pushing her towards Kade.

Amber barely had time to see wide open blue eyes and a mouth opening to scream, before Kade disappeared with her. "We have to get back to our castle, now." The girl might be shorter than Kade and had a slight frame, but Amber had learned that a dragon's instinct was to fight. The girl wouldn't remain surprised for long.

"Chait's in the Void," Crystal said.

"Chait, get out of the Void," Amber said.

"We only have two Golds. They can't take everyone back at once," Flinn said. "Crystal goes first."

Amber nodded, turning to Chait. "You heard."

Chait shook his head. "My orders are to watch you."

"The longer we stand around arguing, the greater the chance someone might come across us. We're surrounded by enemy clans." Amber couldn't remember seeing a single ally of theirs on the map Ronan had spread out.

"I will watch her. Return immediately," Rian said. When Chait started to argue, Rian interrupted. "Flinn gets the first trip for his mage, that means he will be the last to leave. Now go before we are discovered. Those dragons we attacked are probably regrouping by now."

Chait nodded. "Who does Turi take?"

Amber didn't have to think twice. "Jay."

Jasper opened his mouth, snapped it shut then opened it again. "Be careful."

Amber nodded, watching as the four disappeared. She scanned the area, finding only small animals hiding. "There's no one around here." She thought of the girl who'd been watching them from the Void. "Unless they're Gold."

Chait and Turi came back out of the Void and this time they took Amber and Maira, leaving them at the front of Temolae Keep. It didn't take Amber long to locate Kade and the girl. She ran inside, stopping in the corridor where Kade warily watched the girl who'd drawn a sword, the keep's soldiers blocking her retreat in the other direction.

Amber stopped near Kade, whose sword was still sheathed. She warily watched the girl. "Who are you?"

The girl kept her sword up, golden hair hanging past her shoulders in a plait that had partially come undone. "He better not expect me to let you live if you try and kill me."

"Who?" Amber took a step forward, feeling Crystal and Jasper join Kade.

"My father. But I don't think he realises how strong you are. I do. I watched you fight. They didn't stand a chance."

"Who are you?" Amber met the blue eyes, trying to figure out why they seemed so familiar.

"Don't forget I saved your life. You owe me for that." The girl lowered her sword.

"We're not planning to hurt you unless you hurt us. We just wanted to know who you are and why you've been watching us," Amber said.

"Is this the one you saw when we were out hunting?" Kade asked Amber.

"Yeah." Then she spoke aloud. "Well?"

"I was curious. He's so weak. He has no way to defend himself. A dragon child is more powerful than him. I want you to turn him into a Dragon Mage like you," the girl said.

"Who." Amber was beginning to get annoyed by the lack of information. Why couldn't the girl come straight out and say who she was?

"My father."

"Roger."

Amber turned towards Jasper, who'd spoken, her mouth dropping open as she met his blue eyes. "Our cousin?" She turned back to face the girl, seeing the similarities now. "You're our cousin?"

Jasper stepped up beside Amber, staring at the girl. "What's your name?"

"Shylah." She paused. "Well? What about my

father? Will you turn him into a mage so he can defend himself? A mage like you three, not those other weak creatures."

"I–" Before Amber could say anything else, Rian interrupted.

"She will need to talk it over with everyone involved. It is not a decision she can make on her own."

Amber nodded her head. Rian's explanation sounded a lot better than her 'I don't know' would have been.

"So I can go and you'll send someone with an answer?" Shylah asked.

Amber looked towards Rian, the same words as before were all she could think to say.

"I will show you to a guest room." Rian took a step forward, his hand outstretched. "Give you time to freshen up before you join us for dinner."

"I'm a prisoner?" Shylah demanded.

"No. You have asked a very big favour of Amber. She will need to know more details to be able to answer the questions that all the others who are involved will have," Rian said.

"I did save her life."

"There were plenty of others around who could

have done the same. Now are you staying or going?" Rian asked.

Shylah looked at each of them warily. "I can go if I want?"

Rian nodded. "But if you leave, your request will not be considered."

Amber wished she had Rian's ability to know what to say. She waited for Shylah's answer.

"All right." Shylah eyed the hand still stretched towards her. "I'll follow you."

Rian dropped his hand, a smile fleetingly appearing. "I will walk beside you." He stepped forward and at a nod from him, the soldiers parted so he and Shylah could walk down the corridor.

As soon as they were out of sight, Amber turned to Jasper. "What are we going to do?"

Jasper shrugged. "I don't know."

She was almost relieved to find she wasn't the only one who couldn't think of anything other than those words to speak. "We have to do something."

"We're not the only mages now," Crystal said.

"We still shouldn't be making any more until after Ronan's lands are taken," Kade said.

"None should be made. The ones we faced today were bad enough. Think what would happen if they'd been able to fly. No dragon would be safe," Flinn said. "We'd all risk turning feral in battle."

"What if we made ones that couldn't fly?" Brann suggested.

"That seems cruel. What if they fell?" Crystal asked.

Flinn pointed an accusing finger at her. "You stay out of it. You're not helping."

Crystal's hands went to her hips. "Don't tell me what to do."

"Why don't we wait for Ronan?" Jasper asked.

"I don't trust him," Flinn growled.

"No one does," Kade said. "But he's our ally. We need to consult him too."

"Good, that's settled," Jasper said. "Amber and I need to make a phone call. We'll see everyone later."

Amber nearly groaned. Ringing her mother was the last thing she wanted to do, but there was no point in putting it off. That'd only make her mother worse to talk to when they did finally ring her.

Chapter Nineteen

Dinner took far too long to eat between Shylah's evasive answers and pleas to have her father become a mage and Flinn's sullen comments. Several times Amber was tempted to throw something at him. Preferably the knives from the table. When the meal ended and Shylah agreed to stay the night, Amber wasn't sure if she should ring Ronan and ask him to come and give his opinion. Should they let a possible enemy stay the night? She had no idea and wasn't sure if disturbing Ronan when he was in the middle of an interrogation was a good idea. In the end, she decided to go to bed and send Ronan a text message in the morning.

When she woke the next morning, the first thing she did was check where everyone was. Shylah wasn't in the guest room she'd been shown to. Slipping out of bed, she shook her head when Kade turned human and raised his head to look at her. She didn't need him following her. Shylah wasn't about to hurt her when she needed something from her. Hopefully. She grabbed her phone from the bedside drawers, sliding it into a pocket as she left the room.

Amber found Shylah in the gardens, sitting on the edge of a large fountain, trailing her fingers in the water.

Shylah watched her warily. "I thought you'd be more like him."

"Like who?"

"My father. He seems to think family is extremely important. Still talks about his little sister who followed him around everywhere. But he had to promise never to contact them to keep them safe. You're not like him. You don't think family is everything."

She struggled to figure out what to tell Shylah. "I would do anything for my family. But it's more than just my brother and parents. There's Crystal, Kade and Rian too. And many more, but you don't need the full list."

"So I'm not family?"

Amber shrugged. "I don't know. You dragons think differently." Ronan would be proud of how cautious she was being, but she hated it. This was her cousin. She wanted to like her, wanted to be able to trust her. Why did dragons have to ruin everything? "You're the one who came to me for help and yet every question I asked you last night you sidestepped it, avoided it or turned it back at me. Maybe I should be the one to ask if you're family."

"You were trying to figure out our strengths."

"I–" Amber shook her head. "What?"

"You wanted to know about my blood sisters, my parents, my clan. You were trying to find out our strengths and weaknesses."

Amber stared at the girl, her eyes so much like Jasper's. "This is why I don't trust you. I wanted to know about my family. Our family. You don't want me to know them. You kept pushing me away last night. You've been raised on survival of the fittest. I've been raised to look out for family and friends, protect those weaker than me. You want to kill those weaker."

"If you don't take them out when they're weaker they might take you out if they ever become stronger."

"Then why did you try and save me yesterday?"

"So you'd owe me a favour. I need to make my father strong. I shouldn't have to always protect him.

One day someone will capture him and they'll try and use him against me."

She thought of Ronan who'd remove the issue before it became a problem. "Doesn't survival of the fittest count for him?"

Shylah looked away. It was a full minute before she answered. "I owe him."

"What do you owe him?"

Shylah jumped to her feet, crossing the short distance between them. "What does it matter?" There was anger in her voice as she glared at Amber.

"You want my help, remember. What do you owe him?"

"Nothing." Shylah spat the word at her. "They raised me to think like you do. To protect the weak. They didn't raise me right. I need to be stronger than that. One day I'll have to take care of the clan. I can't afford to look after the weak. They'll bring me down and the entire clan with me."

Amber forced herself to hold her ground when all she wanted to do was step back from the anger pouring off Shylah. "If you don't owe him, then what?"

"I love him." She spoke the words in the same tone as someone would say 'I hate him'.

"Maybe you are family after all."

"I'm… I'm family?" The anger faded from Shylah's voice. "You'll help him?"

"I can't promise anything, but I'm thinking about it. And I'll probably have to meet him." She wanted to meet him anyway. A man who should have been a Knight, but instead married a dragon.

"He can't seek out any of his human family."

Amber grinned. "I'm a Dragon Mage." She might consider herself human, but no one else seemed to.

Shylah nodded. "I need to check on the wording of his promise, but I'm pretty certain it was worded human family." She hesitated. "Can I leave?"

"How will I get in touch with you?"

"I have a phone." Shylah pulled a mobile phone from her pocket.

Amber laughed. "That's the last thing I expected, but I shouldn't be surprised since nearly all the other dragons I know seem to carry one." She withdrew her own phone. "What's your number?" She entered the numbers as Shylah rattled them off. Then she told Shylah her number.

"Now can I go?"

Amber nodded. She had no reason to keep her here and she had to let her go sometime. It wasn't like she was really a prisoner. "I'll ring you in a few days. I need to talk to all my allies."

With a nod, Shylah disappeared into the Void.

Amber stared at the place she'd been, wishing she could see into the Void like Crystal could. She looked at her phone in her hand and decided it was probably past time to send Ronan a message. Sitting on the edge of the fountain she typed in the message, deleting it several times before she was happy with what she'd written. As soon as it was sent, she returned her phone to her pocket, continuing to sit on the edge of the fountain.

She closed her eyes, listening to the fall of water. It should be a soothing sound, but it only reminded her of secrets. Dragon secrets. Damn dragons ruined everything. Rising to her feet, she started to walk away, freezing and turning around, her hands raised with fireballs at the ready. Ronan stood by the fountain and he didn't look happy. She closed her hands, extinguishing the flames before she lowered them.

Ronan held up his phone, the text from her displayed. "What is this meant to mean? You leave it a day to inform me and you don't even bother ringing. What game are you playing at?"

"None. I was surprised, that's all. And I didn't want to interrupt your interrogation."

"You don't let anyone take you by surprise. You

need to be more prepared than that. Are you trying to get yourself killed?"

Amber shook her head. Maybe she should have sent him a message last night.

"Or do you think you can keep running to me every time you're in trouble? I'm not your warrior."

"I don't think that." Or at least she wasn't about to admit it to him, not with how angry he looked.

Ronan grabbed hold of her arm, pulling her close. "You are not to make any more mages. Are you trying to help our enemies? Look what happened when you let Shannon in on some of the secret. You nearly got us killed."

"Did you find her?"

"She's dead. They killed her because she couldn't tell them exactly how to make mages." Ronan let Amber go, taking a step away from her.

Thinking he was about to leave, she reached for him, being dragged into the Void and to a room she didn't recognise. "Where are we?" She mentally searched the area, but nothing seemed familiar and the tug of her family and friends was faint. She began to think he wasn't going to speak.

"I've outlasted them all."

There was only one exit, a large timber door with metal hinges reaching halfway across it. The stone walls were covered in small brass plaques. Amber crossed the room to get a closer look. She ran her fingers over the name before she turned to face Ronan. "Where are we?"

He stared at her silently for several minutes. "My family crypt. They're all ashes. Not a single one of my family became a Knight trophy. And I've outlasted them all. My grandparents, their parents, my parents and my sister. Sons that failed me, my uncle, even he I wouldn't leave for anyone else. There'll be more. I won't end up in here." He pointed a finger at her, anger in his tone. "I won't let your decisions put me in here."

"Sons that failed you? How?"

"By dying."

"I don't plan on dying." How could she? The moment she was dead all her friends and family were in danger.

"Humans are such insignificant creatures. If you weren't useful we wouldn't bother letting you live." He stalked across the room, coming to a stop in front of her. "I don't know how you've managed to stay alive as long as you have."

"Because I'm too stubborn to die." She met his hard stare. "I have too many people to take care of to let myself die. You might see them as a liability, I see them as the reason I survive."

"You won't be making any more mages. When we take out the ones Shannon was forced to make, and those with the knowledge, there'll be no others that aren't completely ours."

Amber shook her head. "I will agree to that only until your lands are captured."

"So you've made up your mind. Why did you bother asking for my advice?"

"I need to know more about my uncle and his clan before I can make a proper decision. But I'm not spending the rest of my life as a rare commodity. If every clan had a Dragon Mage then things would be different. No one would have an advantage and we'd cease to be hunted."

"Fool." He sent her a look of disgust. "You will always be hunted. The strongest always are."

She shrugged, not bothering to argue with him. "Where did they get the people from to turn them into mages?"

"A convention for, as the prisoner put it, fantasy geeks. Whatever that is meant to mean."

"That makes sense. They're people who wish they could be mages."

"They are weak and useless. Saying the word

torture was all it took for one of them to spill all his secrets along with every boring detail of his extremely uninteresting life."

"Who made him?"

"He doesn't know, but if I take him to his home he'll be able to get everything he needs to create their images and that of the castle he was held at. His computer with some drawing programs and a drawing tablet. He calls himself an artist and yet he can't use pen and paper."

"I want to see him. Both of them."

"No."

"Yes."

"They're pathetic creatures. I'm not having you feel sorry for them."

"I want to see them. They don't belong to you."

Ronan smiled his predatory smile. "But they are in my keeping."

"I won't be the only one who'll want to see them."

"You have more than enough people to protect. You don't need any more." Ronan grabbed hold of her arm, taking her through the Void and back to the fountain. He pointed a finger at her as he stepped away. "No more mages."

This time he vanished before she could stop him. "Bloody dragon," she muttered as she stalked back inside. She mentally searched for him, smiling grimly when she found his direction. He couldn't live in the Void and she knew how to find him. After school tomorrow she'd start. He wasn't keeping her from seeing their prisoners. She wasn't an idiot. She wasn't about to adopt anyone else. There were more than enough people for her to look after already. And she wasn't about to let him think he could ditch her whenever he felt like it. She would find him no matter where he went.

Chapter Twenty

Amber glared at Kade as they came out of the Void into a dimly lit park. "That took us further away. It was completely the wrong direction."

Kade growled. "What did you expect? I've barely started learning the pathways through the Void. Did you think it's automatic? Do you know the streets of every town in your country?"

"Of course not. That'd be impossible."

"Then why would you expect me to know paths to everywhere through the Void?"

"Sorry." She looked away from him. "I just don't want to waste the time we've got. We've already wasted two days." Her mother hadn't wanted to let her out of her sight so they'd enlisted Gary's help. He'd been reluctant, but Amber had told him she'd be going anyway and there'd be a big argument. He'd agreed to take her mother to dinner Wednesday night and Friday night. She was hoping they'd only need tonight to find Ronan, but so far it was taking a lot longer than she'd expected.

"We could force him to take us to the prisoners."

Amber shook her head. "I want to show him I can find him. I want him to know he can't hide from me."

Kade laughed softly.

"What?"

"Dragon." He said the word affectionately.

"I'm not. I'm human."

"Uh-huh."

"Take me back to the last place. At least it was closer to Ronan than this is."

Kade took them through the Void to the last place they'd been. An empty alley with overflowing industrial bins. "He won't be happy to have you track him down. It might even turn him against you in the long run."

"He thinks he can disappear when he no longer needs me and I won't be able to go to him for help. I want to show him that's not an option. I'm not some weak human he can ditch when I'm no longer useful. He needs to learn that now."

Kade chuckled. "I think he's already starting to realise you're not weak. Just be careful tonight. He won't be the only one there. He'll have guards."

Pulling out her phone, she checked the time. "Fly me. Going through the Void isn't getting us there quick enough."

"I thought you wanted to be back before your mum gets home."

Amber shrugged. "So I'll be in trouble again. This is more important." It was probably a crazy idea to track Ronan down, but she wasn't about to let him tell her what she could and couldn't do. It was a matter of survival. She thought of her brother and Crystal and everyone else who was important to her. She didn't have a choice. Not if she wanted to keep them safe. Ronan had to believe she was just as strong as him. "Come on, fly me there."

"We don't have a saddle."

"I'll manage." She grinned. "Besides, if I fall I can always turn into a goshawk."

Kade shook his head and stared at her for a moment before he turned into a dragon. Amber scrambled up onto his back, leaning forward to hold on with her arms, pressing her knees into him. He took to the air and Amber directed him, as she continued to search out Ronan. It took several hours to reach their destination, a warehouse on the Sunshine Coast, in an industrial area.

Amber slid off Kade's back, her arms and legs

trembling from holding on tight for so long. Using her healing ability, she stopped the trembling while she checked who was in the area. It was quiet and dark, several people inside the single storey, aluminium clad building. Two humans, four dragons and Ronan.

"What's the plan?" Kade asked.

"To not get killed." She pulled out her phone and dialled Ronan's number.

He answered on the first ring. "No."

"Why are you in such a bad mood?"

"Did you actually have something decent to say or did you ring to pester me again?"

"I've come to see the prisoners. Can you get someone to let me in?" She stepped up to a metal door and knocked on it. The phone disconnected and she spun as she felt Ronan appear behind her.

"How did you find me?"

Grinning, Amber slid her phone into her pocket. "I told you I could."

"Can you find anyone you want?"

She shook her head. "Only people I know well."

Ronan pointed a finger at her. "You don't know me." He reached out, grabbed her arm and took her inside the building through the Void.

"What about Kade?"

"I've sent someone for him."

Amber was relieved when he appeared in the room. The relief was short lived when she saw it was Alsandair. He was smiling, Kade wasn't. *"Are you okay?"*

"Just get it over with, Amber. Gary sent me a message to say they're home and your mum's livid. Expect a call from her any minute."

She quickly pulled out her phone and turned it off before returning it to her pocket. She faced Ronan. "I want to see the prisoners."

With a single nod, Ronan strode from the small plywood clad room and into the large open space of the warehouse. On the other side of the warehouse was another plywood clad room, Tory standing guard at the closed door. He opened the door before they reached it, stepping out of the way.

Inside, one of the prisoners sat with his head bent over a computer as he worked on drawing a face using his drawing tablet. It was the mage who'd formed a ball of ice for the official the day they'd captured him. His desk was a stained timber table, the chair a fold out one that had peeling vinyl hanging in strips. In the corner, on the floor, sat the other prisoner, his arms wrapped around his legs as he rocked back and forth.

"I've nearly-" the man looked up from his computer, his words stopping abruptly when he saw them. He scrambled to his feet, backing away as his gaze flickered to each of them. A skinny man with long black hair tied at the nape of his neck and fear in his brown eyes. "I can't go any faster. But I'm nearly there. You promised me. You promised." His gaze momentarily darted to Ronan before it returned to Amber.

"What did you say to him?" Amber demanded of Ronan.

Ronan grinned. "Apparently you give him nightmares. He has a bit of an issue with you letting him fall to his death."

"Why didn't you tell me?" Amber asked.

"You promised me." The man couldn't back away any further, he was against the wall. The other prisoner at his feet continued to rock back and forth.

"I told you that you couldn't see them. You wouldn't listen."

Amber tried to keep the anger from her voice when she spoke to the man pressed against the wall. "I'm sorry, but it was a battle. This is different. I'm not going to hurt you."

"Unless he tries to escape," Ronan said.

Amber shot Ronan a glare before she turned back to the prisoner. "What's your name?"

"Cooper."

"And your friend?"

Cooper looked down at the man at his feet. "I never knew him before they brought us all together. That's Miles." He continued to remain pressed against the wall.

"What do I say to him? How do I make him stop being afraid?" She sent the thought to Kade.

"You're asking the wrong person."

Amber held back a sigh. "Look, Cooper, I don't plan to kill you. We just need to know everything you know about the people who recruited you. I'm only here to make sure that you're being treated okay. Dragons don't always know how to deal with us humans."

"I didn't know. None of us knew. We didn't expect this. We thought it'd be fun. When they turned into dragons we were amazed. It was like a dream come true. Then it became a nightmare."

"We? How many of you were there?" Amber asked.

Cooper came away from the wall slightly. "Six. The first one they put the blood on his hands. His palms were red with it when he took the Pliethin.

Shannon kept saying they didn't take that much blood from her. That she could smell it on Jasper, but not that much. It didn't work. They were so angry they slit his throat in front of us and there was blood all over the floor. I don't even remember his name." He shuddered, falling silent.

"Why did they only send four of you against us if they had five?" Kade asked.

Cooper shook his head. "They gave him too much dragon blood to drink. That's what they tried next. Within minutes of drinking it he was on the ground clutching at his stomach, screaming. He started coughing up blood, still screaming. Then he was quiet." Cooper covered his face with his hands. "They still made us drink it. Shannon kept saying you only took a couple of drops from her. This time it was a teaspoon instead of half a glass. I waited for it to kill me, but it didn't. They kept asking her how you'd made the mages and she kept saying she didn't know. Kept telling them she was blindfolded." He uncovered his face. "Don't make me go back there. Please."

Amber tried to feel nothing for Cooper, but she ached to comfort him. She hated when Ronan was right. "I–"

Ronan interrupted. "I've already told you. Until the

ones who made you are dead, you belong to them. Get the drawings done and we'll deal with them."

"Then I can go back to my old life? I can forget all about this and go home?"

"How many times do I have to tell you that your problems will be over once they're dead?" Ronan asked irritably.

Amber's gaze narrowed. *"You better not be planning to kill him."*

"You can't have him. You can't adopt every single stray."

"I don't want him. But I'm not going to let you kill him."

"You can't let him go back to his old life. He might tell someone."

"He won't. I'll make sure of it. Both of them will be helped to return to their old lives."

"What's wrong? Why isn't anyone saying anything?" Cooper asked. He looked at each of them.

"I was thinking," Amber said. "How old are you?" She sent her thoughts to Ronan. *"I'm serious. No killing either of them."*

"Miles has already tried to kill himself twice. I don't know why Cooper bothered saving him. A waste of time," Ronan told Amber.

"Twenty."

He was only two years older than her brother.

Barely an adult. She had no idea how to save him, not if Ronan really wanted to kill him. She couldn't afford to claim another one. Eventually, Ronan would say enough and then there might be someone else she needed to protect even more. "Where do you live?"

"In Brisbane. In my parents' home. I've got an older brother who lives with us too." He sounded defensive.

"Ronan's right. We need to find out who will be looking for you. Without names, we're working in the dark. We'll do everything possible to help you get your life back to normal, but you have to know that some things are going to always be different." She looked down at his hands. Lifting her own she momentarily called flames to them. "Some things can't be undone."

Cooper seemed to sag. "I just want it to be the same as it used to be. I want the nightmares to end and I want to forget this ever happened. And I want Miles to stop staring into space and rocking like that all the time. It's driving me crazy. He's a couple of years older than me. Why can't he cope?"

"Age means nothing," Kade said. "You won't end up like him."

"How can you know that?" There was fear and a sound of desperation in Cooper's voice.

"Because you're talking to us right now."

Cooper stared at Kade a moment before he nodded his head.

It was another couple of hours before they were finally able to leave. Cooper had wanted more reassurances and Ronan had wanted Kade to see if any of the images Cooper was in the process of drawing looked familiar. None did. Before they returned to Kade's room, Amber warned Ronan once more not to kill their prisoners. The predatory smile he gave her didn't reassure her in the least.

When they arrived home, Kade sent Brann to tell Amber's mother that they were already asleep and would see her in the morning. Amber dropped onto the bed, wishing it was true, but it didn't take long for exhaustion to overtake her and she fell into dreams filled with blood. This time it was blood creeping across the floor, coming closer and closer no matter how far she retreated.

The sound of the bedroom door opening had Amber sitting up, launching a fireball before she could register it was her mother in the doorway. At the same time Kade turned into his human form and disappeared into the Void, reappearing in front of Donna who was screaming.

Swearing, Amber threw herself across the room as

the fireball impacted with Kade's back, pressing her hands against him as she healed him. "I'm sorry. I'm so sorry." Keeping a hand on Kade, she reached out to hug her mother with a single arm. "You shouldn't have come in here like that. I was asleep. I didn't know it was you." She could feel the tremble in her mother's body. "Say something, Mum."

Donna's mouth opened, then closed.

"Mum?"

"I thought I got here in time. She didn't get hit, did she?" Kade eyed Donna.

"Mum?" She let go of Kade to take her mother's hand, still keeping her arm around her. "Maybe you should get Gary."

"I sent Brann for him."

Maira entered the hallway stopping in the doorway behind Donna. "Can I help? Is she okay?" There was the sound of running footsteps and Gary and Brann joined her.

"Donna?" Gary tugged her away from Amber, sliding an arm around her waist. "Come back to our room and I'll check you over."

They were partway down the hallway before Donna pulled away from him. She met Amber's gaze. "You're grounded."

Amber laughed, running forward to throw her arms around her mother. "I love you."

Donna hugged her tightly. "You're still grounded."

"No, I'm not."

"This isn't up for discussion."

"Are we going to school today?" Maira asked. "Because if we are, we better get ready or we're going to be late."

Amber pulled away from her mother, then stepped forward again to hug her fiercely. "Never do that again. Knock first. And I'm not grounded." She strode back to the bedroom.

"For a month," Donna called after her.

Amber closed the door as soon as Kade was in the room and her smile faded as she sagged against the door. Kade drew her close, wrapping his arms around her. "Thank you for saving my mum."

"Maybe I should have Brann and Maira take turns at guarding the door."

"I thought she'd be safe here." Amber couldn't keep the images from her dream out of her mind. The last thing she needed was a return of her nightmares. "I thought I could keep her safe." Over and over she saw the fireball headed for her mother.

"Do you want me to find somewhere else for her to stay?"

"I don't know."

"You don't have to decide straight away."

She couldn't kick her mother out. Actually, she doubted she'd go. Maybe she could send her to stay with her brother. That thought nearly brought a smile to her lips. He'd probably kill her. What her mother needed was something to keep her from interfering. Something time consuming. Like a job. Amber thought of Miles, rocking in the corner. "I've got it."

"Are you going to share?"

Amber grinned. "It's perfect. Right up Gary's alley."

Kade laughed. "The prisoner who lost his mind."

"Yeah. Miles."

There was a tap on the bedroom door. "Breakfast is ready," Maira called out.

"We'll be there shortly," Kade called before he lowered his voice. "Do you want me to get Maira to organise it?"

Amber shook her head. "I'll ask Rian. He'll probably do a better job at convincing mum than anyone else would." She drew away from Kade, fireballs ready when she felt someone step out of the Void and into the bedroom. Her heart raced as she remembered the sensation of throwing fireballs at her mother. "Will everyone stop bursting in on me like this?"

"Chait said you tried to kill your mother."

Amber glared at him, extinguishing the fire. "It was an accident."

"Don't screw up. I don't need you ending up as useless as Miles."

"About Miles."

"What are you planning? I don't like that look you've got in your eye."

Amber laughed, trying to act normal. She couldn't show Ronan any weakness. No matter how close to losing it she felt right now. "I think you'll love it. Not only will it get Miles out of your way, it'll keep my mum from messing with your plans as often."

"Spit it out. I haven't got all day."

Neither did she, not if she wanted to get to school on time. Maybe she didn't need to, but Kade should if he didn't want to draw unwanted attention.

Chapter Twenty-One

The past week had been busy. Rian had arranged a place in town for Donna and Gary to stay at with Miles. Donna had readily agreed to help Miles when she saw the condition he was in. The downside was that she now expected Amber and Jasper to end up in the same state. Amber had rung Shylah on the weekend and said that she couldn't even think about helping Roger until after Ronan's lands had been returned to him. Shylah had offered to help and was now pestering Amber to take her to meet their grandparents.

Amber kept putting that task off. She didn't need threats against her life to help bring back the nightmares. Instead of telling Shylah about her fears, she promised to take her to visit them the following weekend. On Saturday morning, Amber reluctantly let Kade take her to their castle, where they had agreed to meet Shylah and Ronan. From there they planned to take her to Ronan's place.

Ronan arrived first. "You were too nice to Cooper. The boy is useless now. Complains I make him work too hard. Sleeps ridiculously large amounts of time and still hasn't finished a single drawing. You need to sort him out before I have to. I doubt you'll like the methods I'll use."

"Fine. I'll do it tomorrow."

"After we've been to see your Knights."

Amber shook her head. The last thing she was going to feel like doing was sort out more dramas after seeing her grandparents. "Tomorrow."

"By then I may have removed a limb or two. He doesn't need his legs to draw."

Amber opened her mouth to argue, but Kade interrupted her.

"We'll see how long this takes. Stay away from Cooper for the rest of the day and it won't be a problem."

"The longer it takes him to draw his pictures the more likely it is someone will find him and we'll never know who made him. Do you want that?" Ronan demanded.

This time it was Shylah's arrival that prevented Amber from answering.

"Who's taking me there?" Shylah looked at each of them.

Kade stepped forward. "I am."

Amber moved to Ronan's side. After discussing it with Kade, they'd decided it was the safest option. Ronan needed her, he didn't need Shylah. "I'll meet you there." Her gaze met Kade's and held it for a moment before he nodded and vanished into the Void. She turned to Ronan. "Let's go." With a grin, Ronan took her through the Void, arriving in the plywood room that Cooper was being kept in. "Damn it, Ronan!"

"Deal with him." Ronan stalked out of the room, slamming the door shut behind him.

Cooper leapt up from the mattress on the floor, rubbing at his eyes. "What's happening?"

"Shut up for a minute," Amber growled at him as she pulled out her phone and rang Kade.

"Where are you?"

"Ronan decided Cooper couldn't wait. Don't let Shylah see our grandparents until I get there." Although knowing Ronan, she guessed the door was probably locked.

"Do you want me to come and get you?"

Amber shook her head even though Kade couldn't

see her. "No. I might as well get this over and done with."

"I'll see you soon."

"Yeah." She hung up, returning her phone to her pocket, frowning at Cooper.

He took a step backwards. "What's going on?"

His action annoyed her and she could only imagine how much it must annoy Ronan. "Stop acting so weak. You won't last long if you don't get your act together."

He cringed away from her. "You said you'd protect me."

"I can only do so much. I don't control Ronan. No one does. You need to get the drawings finished before he decides to start removing limbs."

Cooper stumbled to the chair, collapsing onto it. "You said you'd protect me."

She wanted to yell at him, but he looked too fragile. Why had Ronan thought she could deal with Cooper? She was one of the least diplomatic people in the world. "Look, Cooper, you aren't safe here. I can't get you to a safer place until you get those drawings done. This is serious. You're still in danger."

"But no one knows I'm here."

"They can still find you. Trust me on this. I know exactly what I'm talking about."

"How?"

She hesitated. "I had an assassin after me."

"What happened to them?"

"I killed the one who sent the assassin."

Cooper dropped his head into his hands. "I'm dead. I might as well let you kill me now."

She fought the urge to shake him, then wondered what was the point. She recoiled from that idea. There was no way she was going to start thinking like that. She'd obviously been hanging out with dragons too long. Taking a deep breath, she crossed the room and pulled his hands from his face. "You're not dead yet. Now why haven't you finished your drawings?"

"They're not right. I don't want to accuse the wrong people. I don't want the death of an innocent person on my shoulders."

"Okay, you draw your pictures as best as you can. We'll get photos to you of dragons that look like those pictures and you can tell us if that's them. How does that sound?"

"Okay." He spoke hesitantly. "What about the castle where I was kept?"

"Focus on the people first, then the castle. Okay?"

He nodded. When she didn't speak for several minutes, he did. "Now?"

"Of course now. Ronan isn't a patient man. At least not about some things."

Cooper turned in his chair and pulled up one of his images on his computer. He looked over his shoulder. "You're not going to watch me, are you?"

"No." The word was said through gritted teeth. "I'm actually meant to be somewhere else, not here trying to keep Ronan from killing you. As soon as you get this done and we find who made you, you can return to your life."

Panic crossed Cooper's face.

"What now?" She didn't even bother keeping the exasperation she felt from filling her voice.

"How can I do that? I thought I could. I want to. But how can I go back? They'll have questions. The dragons made me send them a message that I was taking off with a girl I'd met at the convention. What do I tell them about her?"

"You don't have to go home if you don't want to."

"Then where do I go instead?" He held out his hands, forming balls of ice in them. "What good will this do me?"

She thought of Kade and Shylah waiting for her. "I don't bloody know. Look, we'll sort it out somehow. You won't be ditched by the side of the road. Is that why you're being so slow? Because you've got nowhere to stay once you're finished here."

"No." Cooper frowned. "I don't think so. I was worried I'd get an innocent person killed."

Good thing he hadn't met any Knights. They'd soon tell him there was no such thing as an innocent dragon. She pushed that thought aside, trying to focus on getting Cooper back to work so she could see her grandparents. Not that she really wanted to see them. "Do you have a phone?"

He nodded. "There isn't much credit left on it."

"That I can deal with." Or at least get Rian to deal with it. She needed easier access to her money. "Get rid of that ice."

Cooper turned his hands like he was about to throw them.

"Stop! What are you doing?"

"Getting rid of them."

"I meant like this." She brought fire to her hands then extinguished it.

"I can't do that. Mine is ice."

"Crystal can."

"Who's Crystal?"

Amber shook her head. "Forget it." She reached out, calling fire to her hands, and melted his ice.

Cooper jumped to his feet, brushing water from his clothes. "What did you do that for?"

"Because you couldn't."

"I'm wet." He stared down at himself.

"Just get back to work."

"You were asking me about my phone."

"Oh, yeah. I'll give you my number." She waited for him to pull out his phone and rattled it off, taking out her own phone when he offered her his number. "Now get back to work. I've got other things to deal with." She didn't wait for his answer, striding from the room as she mentally searched for Ronan. Finding him in the other room, she crossed the warehouse, ignoring the couple of dragons in human form that were guarding the place. Entering the other room, she stayed by the door. "Let's go."

Ronan remained seated in the faded armchair, not looking up from his phone. His finger flicked across the screen. "Did you sort him out?"

"Yes. Now let's go." Her tone was curt.

Ronan finally looked up. "I had him working until you arrived and screwed everything up." He rose to his feet, putting his phone away. "There's no need to take that tone with me, you've only got yourself to blame." He reached for her.

Amber stepped back, almost out of the room. "I

was going to deal with him. Later. Stop dragging me around the countryside for your convenience."

"Are you finished?" His tone was glacial.

She supposed she better be, before she alienated him any further. "Yes." Stepping forward, this time she let Ronan take her arm when he reached for her. They arrived in his house. Kade was sitting in a lounge chair while Shylah paced back and forth in front of him, since most of the space in the lounge room was filled by large comfortable chairs.

Shylah stopped in mid step, turning to face them. "About time. I didn't agree to this. The plan was to come straight here and see my father's parents."

"An emergency came up that needed to be dealt with immediately." Amber ignored the noise Ronan made. It had sounded suspiciously like a snort. "We can see them now." She mentally searched for them, trying to figure out where their new suite was in comparison to the lounge room. Unable to find them, she guessed the new suite was made from the same material as their prison had been.

"This way." Ronan strode from the room and they trailed behind him. He led them to a hallway that ended with a locked, reinforced door. Unlocking it, he swung it open, checking the room before he entered, everyone following him inside.

Charles and Helen were both seated at a large dining table, pages of writing and faded maps spread out between them. On the other side of the room was a pair of armchairs and a television. On the far side of the room were two doors. One was open, showing a king-sized bed. The other was closed.

"About time you got here." Charles looked at the watch he now wore. "In future I expect you to be more punctual."

Amber barely stopped herself from telling him that he didn't have anywhere else to go. "Grandad, Grandma, I want you to meet Shylah. Roger's daughter."

"A dragon," Charles spat the words out, his expression one of disgust.

"Why did you bring her here?" Helen demanded. Her expression mirrored her husband's.

Obviously surprising them with the visit hadn't been a good plan, but letting them know in advance probably wouldn't have helped either. Amber didn't know what to say to them.

"I don't know why he's bothered to protect you two all these years." Shylah's own expression wasn't much better than her grandparents. "He's obviously wasted his time."

Charles jumped to his feet, his chair tipping back before it righted itself. "Lies."

Helen rose slower. "How did he protect us? He was a child."

"When they set him free. He had to promise never to see his human family or they'd be killed."

"Who made him promise?" Charles demanded.

"It doesn't matter. He wasted his time. Just like I've wasted mine." Shylah spun on her heel and started to stride from the room.

Chapter Twenty-Two

"Kade. Grab her." Amber told Kade, who was closest to the door.

"Let me go." Shylah glared at him as she tried to pull away.

"Don't run off," Amber said.

"I wish you lot would stop grabbing me. You'd think after I saved your life in that battle two weeks ago you'd be a little nicer to me." Shylah turned her glare on Amber.

"You didn't save my life. I had plenty of help."

At the same time as Amber spoke, Charles demanded, "What battle?"

"You have us reading all these stupid documents while you've been out there killing dragons?" Helen asked.

Amber nearly swore. It'd have to be a dragon

causing her problems. Yet again. "It was a test. Kade is still doing his warrior tests."

"I don't care what battle it is, you're not leaving us in this prison. We didn't agree to that," Charles said.

"It's not a prison. It's a proper room," Amber argued.

"There are bars on the windows and the door is locked. No matter how you fancy it up, it's still a prison," Helen said. "I can't believe my own granddaughter would do this to me."

"I can't believe my own grandparents threatened to kill me." Amber returned Helen's glare.

"There'll be a battle soon," Ronan said.

"When?" Charles, Helen and Amber all asked at once.

"What battle?" Amber asked, not wanting to sound like her grandparents.

"When your boy finally identifies who made him, we'll hunt them down," Ronan said.

"He's not certain he can get the drawings exact. I told him we'd provide photos of people who look like the images he draws so he can confirm," Amber said.

"People or dragons?" Charles asked. "We're not killing people."

"Dragons," Amber said. Why had she been in such a hurry to leave Cooper? He'd been much easier to deal with than this group. "I'm not sure how long it'll take."

"He better not take too long," Ronan warned.

"Is this why you wouldn't let me leave? You want me to help fight your battles for you?" Shylah asked.

Amber shook her head. "No, I just…" Her voice trailed off. She just was an idiot. Her grandparents weren't about to accept a dragon grandchild anymore than they'd accept a Dragon Mage grandchild. "Never mind."

"She wanted to talk to you about meeting your father," Kade said.

Amber sent him a grateful smile. She'd forgotten about that plan in all the drama. "I'll ring you. We'll set a time later."

"You're going to see Roger?" Helen asked.

"He's not our son," Charles said. "He's a dragon now."

Helen started to speak then closed her mouth, her lips drawing in tight.

"He wants to see you," Shylah said to Amber. "And he asked me to give a message to them." She sent a look of disgust towards Helen and Charles.

"What did he say?" Helen asked.

"It isn't important. He's a dragon," Charles said.

Shylah met Helen's gaze. "He never forgot you.

Ever. He even named his youngest daughter after you." Her gaze shifted to Charles. "His second daughter he named Charlotte for you."

"We don't want dragons named after us. We're Knights," Charles said.

Shylah nodded. "I know. I'm only here because he can't be. If I hadn't made a promise, I'd kill you for all the dragons you've killed."

"Don't let that stop you. Try girl and you'll see I'm not so easy to kill," Charles said.

"No one is killing anyone today," Amber said firmly.

"You've always got to interfere when things start to get interesting."

Ignoring Ronan's words, Amber turned to Shylah. "I'll ring you."

Shylah nodded before she entered the Void.

Amber turned to her grandfather. "Would it have hurt you to be nice? Or at least to not be nasty. She's family."

"She's a dragon. We don't have dragons in our family."

She stared at him, wondering why she'd bothered. He wasn't interested in seeing dragons as anything other than the enemy. She couldn't see how a month with the Knights was going to convince her to join them. Not if they all had the same attitude as her grandfather. "I'll be back when we know who we're to attack."

Charles gestured towards the table. "Then what's all this for?"

"The battle after the next one." She reached out a hand to Kade, but before she could take his hand and ask him to get her out of there, Ronan stepped between them.

"Not so fast, kitten. We've got business to discuss." Ronan gestured towards the door.

"What sort of business?" Helen demanded.

"Nothing to do with either of you. Dragon business." Ronan strode for the door, ignoring Charles' demands that he be told what was going on. He closed the door once Amber and Kade were in the hallway, locking it. Striding back down the hallway, he didn't bother to check if they were following.

"Do you know what it's about?" Kade asked Amber.

"I haven't got a clue." She followed Ronan. "What business?"

Ronan didn't talk until they were back in the lounge room where they'd arrived. "Why does Cooper need pictures?"

"Because he's worried his drawings aren't good enough to figure out the correct people."

"What if I can't get photos of the correct people? They're not about to stand around and smile for the camera."

"I'm sure you'll work it out."

"Don't go making any other deals on my behalf without consulting me."

"I didn't–"

"You made the deal with Cooper about the photos."

"It made sense."

"It doesn't make sense. It's going to slow everything down."

Amber glared at Ronan. "You're the one not making sense."

"Was that all the business you wanted to talk about?" Kade asked.

"Yes. You can go," Ronan said dismissively.

Before Amber could argue, Kade took her back to his house through the Void. "I wasn't finished talking."

"You were wasting your breath."

"Mine to waste."

"Come on, Amber. Did you really want to spend the rest of the day arguing with Ronan? Haven't you got better things to do?"

She thought of the new bracelets sitting on the

bathroom vanity waiting to be filled with power. "Yeah." She strode from the room, ignoring Kade's question of what she was doing. She was sick of people pushing her around. Actually, it was dragons she was sick of. Them and Knights. She was perfectly capable of running her own life without their interference.

* * *

Amber stared at the photos Chait handed her. It was over a week since she'd seen her grandparents, nearly two weeks, and tomorrow was the last day of school before they broke up for the September holidays. "Are these them? The ones who made the mages?"

Chait nodded.

"Does Ronan know who they are?"

Kade came into the kitchen. "What have you got?"

She held the photos out.

Kade stopped at the second photo. "An Elder?" He looked over at Amber. "It's an Elder that's making mages and using details of the tests to hunt us?"

"I don't know." She turned to Chait. "Is it?"

"Ronan said he'd be here soon." Chait disappeared into the Void.

"I hate it when you lot do that." For a moment she stared at the spot where Chait had been before she turned her attention to Kade. "What does it mean if it's an Elder?"

"There are only twenty-five Elders. Beneath them are the Council, then the Assembly, then the Representatives. Elders are the most powerful dragons in all the worlds and the ones who uphold the law more than any other dragon. They are the law and must always be above it."

"Yet he's breaking the law." Amber gestured towards the photo Kade still held. "What does that mean for us?"

"That we need to have proof that's completely inarguable. No one would believe this of an Elder. And each Elder has so many allies that a battle against them is almost guaranteed to be won by them."

"So basically we're screwed."

Ronan stepped out of the Void. "Not even close."

"Then what?" Amber demanded.

"We prove he has not only bent the law, but twisted it out of recognition and not a single one of his allies will stand beside him. Once he's taken care of, there'll be fighting between the Councillors over who moves up and then there'll be a position available on the Council. We don't let anyone know it's an elder until we're completely ready and have inarguable proof. Before then we need to move up the taking of my lands. I don't want someone on the Assembly thinking the position we create is theirs.

"Impossible."

"Don't tell me impossible. You have school holidays starting tomorrow. We can start the day after."

"Why?" Amber asked.

"He wants the Council position," Kade said. "Which Gold Dragon are you backing for the position?"

Ronan smiled. "There will be hell to pay if I don't get it."

Amber shivered at the predatory smile, a flash of gold momentarily appearing in Ronan's eyes. She had a feeling the only dragon he had in mind for the position was himself. "What about the other Dragon Mage and the Elder making them?"

"We can't take them out until I have my lands. I'm not risking things moving too fast for me to get that Council position."

"We aren't ready to attack. It's too soon to be able to win."

"You will be ready. No excuses. My house Saturday morning. All of you. It's time to go over the final plans." Ronan held Amber's gaze a moment longer before he vanished into the Void.

Amber reached for Kade, holding his hand tight. "Can we do it?"

"I hope so."

She shivered again. They were so not ready for this. None of them. The castle's occupants would know what to expect. They had no new battle tactics with which to surprise them like they had at Temolae Keep. "We're screwed."

"So that's it? You're giving up?"

Amber thought of Cooper, covering his face with his hands. Then she thought of her brother, Crystal, her mother, even her grandparents. The images of people that she had claimed filled her mind. She reached out a hand and ran it down Kade's cheek, along his neck, stopping at his heart. It beat strongly beneath her palm. "No. We'll get him his lands." She didn't have a choice.

"We need to let Flinn know."

"Crystal is going to be mad. Her seventeenth birthday is during the September holidays and she was expecting to have a ball to celebrate."

"That's only a week away. Impossible."

Amber grinned. "As impossible as taking Ronan's lands these holidays?"

Kade laughed. "I guess we're having a ball."

Amber joined him, noticing a slight touch of hysteria to the sound of her laugh. "There's no way I'm telling Mum. She'll try and ground me again. We're going to our castle to celebrate Crystal's birthday. Right?"

"Okay."

Amber took a deep breath, trying not to think about what was coming. "This is crazy," she muttered.

"Crazy? Aren't you the one who jumps off my back in mid air?"

"That's different." She eyed his smile, thinking it looked a little bit too much like Ronan's predatory one. "You're looking forward to this, aren't you?"

"I'm a dragon. We live for battle and stealing our neighbour's land."

"Just great." She pulled away from him. "I'm going to ring Crystal. And Jay."

Chapter Twenty-Three

When they arrived at Ronan's house, he led them straight to Charles and Helen's room. Extra timber chairs had been set around the table, which was covered in numerous piles of paper. Amber looked away from the glare her grandfather sent her. Not the best way to start the first day of the school holidays, but she guessed they weren't about to get any better. She sat down at the table, Kade beside her, and looked around at those assembled. Ronan had two of his sons behind him, Hound and Tory, while Rian stood behind her. Flinn and Crystal were seated, his warriors behind him. Jasper was also at the table and Maira and Brann were seated, much to Flinn's annoyance.

"I only have two people in the castle. I'd planned to have more, but time doesn't allow it," Ronan said.

"Going to war half prepared will get everyone

killed," Charles said. "Not that I care about the rest of you. Die if you want. But you're not endangering me and Helen."

"Circumstances have changed. It was necessary to move our plans forward," Ronan said.

Amber could just imagine how little her grandparents would appreciate helping Ronan get his own Council position. Flinn had been argumentative enough. At least until Kade had pointed out that it wasn't guaranteed. Ronan still had to fight for it and win it for whichever Gold he was sponsoring.

"What circumstances?" Helen asked.

"Future changes in dragon alliances. We need to attack now before those alliances finish changing," Ronan said.

"Are they strengthening their position?" Charles asked.

"Forget the politics for the moment. Focus on strategy. We'll attack at night," Ronan said.

Amber nearly groaned when Charles argued against that plan. Minutes passed as the table erupted into arguments, finally agreeing, reluctantly by some, to attack at night. It was going to be a long day. She eyed the door, wishing she could leave.

"My people will create two separate diversions. One will light a fire-"

Charles interrupted Ronan. "That's too obvious. The first thing they'll think of is attackers."

Amber felt like throttling her grandfather when his words caused another argument to start. Both Ronan and Charles ended up on their feet, shouting at each other over the table before the argument was finished. The decision was reached that one would light a fire in the stables, chasing out the horses, while the other spy set dynamite at the rear wall to make the enemy think they'd be entering through it.

"We'll send a small force towards the back while a larger one attacks from the front and a handful flies in from the side to track down the leaders," Ronan said.

"Where do you think you're going to put us? It better not be in the suicide group attacking the rear," Charles said.

"You'll go where I put you," Ronan roared, rising to his feet again.

Charles leapt to his feet too. "If you think you can get us killed in this battle-"

Amber jumped to her feet. "Stop it! Both of you. We've got no chance of winning if we continue to fight amongst ourselves. Save it for the enemy."

"Don't you talk to me like that, girl." Charles glared at her.

"Well, if you can stop acting like little kids we

won't all end up in-" Her mouth dropped open. "Oh."

"What?" Ronan asked.

Her lips slowly curved into a smile. "A grave."

"Can't see how that can cheer you up," Charles growled. "Unless it was him." He nodded towards Ronan.

Amber met Ronan's gaze. "The crypt."

Ronan grinned.

This time his predatory smile didn't make fear race through her veins. It made her think that they actually had a chance of surviving. "Do they ever have guards in there?"

Ronan shook his head. "What's the point? It's locked. But I can bring warriors in there and we can use some dynamite to blow it open."

"No. Too dangerous. How is it locked?"

"By a key that used to be kept in the library. In the bottom drawer of the desk." Ronan pulled the map towards himself. "Here. This room on the second floor."

"Doesn't mean it'll still be there," Charles said.

"One of the mages could fly in and get it," Maira said.

"Not my mage," Flinn growled.

"I'll do it," Amber said quickly before another argument could start.

"You don't have to," Kade said.

Who else was she going to let do it? Jay? Crystal? No way. "My plan. I'll do it."

"It'll all have to be done at once," Ronan said.

Amber met his gaze. "Everything?"

"If you can't get the key in time I'll be blowing the door open. Obviously I won't be using as much as I would for the outside wall," Ronan said.

Her stomach lurched. It still sounded too dangerous. "Once I get the key, how do I get it to you?"

Ronan continued to meet her gaze. "Call for me and I'll find you."

She wasn't certain if that was a threat or a promise. She nodded, hoping it was a promise. "Then we can attack from inside."

"We'll have the advantage," Ronan said.

"We're going with the group attacking from inside," Charles ordered.

"So are we," Flinn stated.

Amber held her breath, expecting more arguments. Instead, Ronan nodded. Her gaze travelled around the table and she stared intently at everyone there. Apart from Flinn and his warriors she'd be devastated if something happened to one of them. Possibly not her grandfather, but she wasn't certain. Her gaze was drawn to Ronan. She'd even be devastated if something happened to him. And that thought scared the hell out of her more than her fear of losing any of her family or friends. She didn't know what Ronan was, but somehow or other, he'd become one of hers.

Plans and suggestions continued to be thrown around the table, there were more arguments and Amber's gaze kept being drawn back to Ronan, the sense of horror not leaving her. When talking was done, and everyone started to leave, Ronan cornered her in the hallway.

"I need to talk to you."

Amber shot a look to Kade who waited for her, nearly everyone else gone other than Rian. She'd wanted to spend time with Crystal, but they'd all be at their castle tomorrow. Not that they'd probably have much time to chat with everything that still needed to be done.

"Now, Amber."

She knew that tone. It wasn't one to be argued with. "Kade, take Rian to Temolae Keep and come back for me."

"No need. I'll take her to your house when I'm finished talking to her," Ronan said.

"Okay." She was surprised that none of her worry leaked into the tone of her voice.

"Are you sure?" Kade asked Amber.

"Yes. He still needs me. I'll be fine." She tried to sound reassuring, but wasn't certain if she managed to convey that feeling.

Kade nodded, reaching for Rian before he disappeared into the Void.

"This way." Ronan led her to a water garden he'd recently installed in his rooftop garden, indicating an outdoor timber chair she could sit on before sitting on one himself. "What's going on?"

Amber sat down. "I don't know what you mean."

"What are you planning?"

"Nothing."

"Don't lie to me, Amber. I saw those looks you kept sending me. What are you planning?"

She jumped to her feet, started to pace, stopped, faced Ronan then looked away again. There was no way she could get out of telling him what she was thinking. Although he probably wouldn't believe her. "You're crazy."

"I know what I saw."

She shook her head. "No. You're psychotic. A killer. Can't be trusted. I don't want you to be one of mine." The last was a wail.

Ronan rose to his feet, standing directly in front of her. "What exactly are you saying?"

"The battle." She thought of her feelings when she'd looked around the table and feared that she might lose one of them.

"You're not backing out are you?"

"I don't want to lose anyone in it." She hesitated. "Not even you."

"Don't tell me this is the part where you confess your undying love for me." His tone dripped sarcasm.

"No. Most of the time I hate you. And there's a few times I've even wanted to murder you, but the moment passes pretty quickly." She thought of everything that had happened to him. Like his uncle killing his family and trying to kill him. At times she even pitied him, but there was no way she'd ever tell him that.

"Is this a warning?"

She frowned. "A warning?"

"That you will kill me."

She laughed. How was she making such a mess of this? "No. I'm trying to tell you you're one of mine. I will protect you as fiercely as I'd protect Rian."

"Why?"

She smiled ruefully. "Because I'm an idiot."

He grabbed her chin, tilting her head up. "I think you might actually be serious."

She jerked her head out of his hand. "That doesn't mean I'll let you hurt any of my people. You are at the bottom of the list of the ones I'd protect." She pointed a finger at him in warning.

"Why are you telling me this? What's your agenda?"

Amber sighed heavily. "Stop being such a dragon and complicating things. This is human."

"Humans are irrational."

"I know." A wry grin formed.

"This doesn't make sense."

She laughed, this time amused. "Of course it doesn't. It has nothing at all to do with sense. It's to do with being human."

"Would you avenge me if someone killed me?"

Amber shook her head. "I don't think so. That's a dragon emotion. No, this is about protecting and not letting someone kill you in the first place."

"I don't need anyone to protect me."

"Don't you?"

Ronan scowled. "I don't trust you, if that's what you're angling for."

"No. You shouldn't trust me because I will put

everyone else before you. Kade, Crystal, Jay, even Rian. But you are one of mine."

Ronan stared at her, his expression clearing, his predatory smile appearing. "You don't like it."

"No."

"I'll take you home."

She stepped back before he could take her arm. "What are you thinking? Why are you smiling?"

"I don't like that I'm stuck protecting you. It's only fair that you should be stuck with the same feelings."

She was still laughing when Ronan deposited her on Kade's doorstep and vanished back into the Void.

Chapter Twenty-Four

Amber fought to remain calm. She sat down on the edge of a chair, then rose almost immediately. Everyone else had been taken from the planning room. She was the last one Ronan would need to transport. Everything else was in place. His two people were ready to create their diversions. Armies were ready to fly in as soon as they were given the word and Ronan had taken the last person to the crypt. His son Rian.

It was hard to believe that three days ago they'd started planning this battle. Now they were about to fight it. How did Ronan expect them to be ready for this? It was crazy.

She tried to sit down again, but she couldn't stay still. What was taking him so long? When he stepped out of the Void, she jumped slightly.

"Ready?"

She nodded, unable to say anything.

"Are you certain you can do this?"

She forced herself to speak. "Yes."

Ronan reached for her, taking her through the Void to the countryside near his castle. He pointed straight ahead. "The window is directly across from us."

She could barely see anything in the shadowy night. "Okay."

"Let me know what you find when you get in there."

"Okay."

He grabbed her arm again, tightening his grip as he turned her to face him. "Are you certain you can do this?"

Some of her fear was replaced by anger and she dragged her arm away from him. "Yes!"

"About bloody time. You sounded like you'd already lost. Now get in there and get the key."

"This is definitely one of those moments where I feel like murdering you." She glared at him even though he was little more than a shadowy figure.

"The feeling will pass. Or so I've been told." He grinned fleetingly. "Now stop wasting time. Do you want your people to be caught?"

She didn't bother replying. Turning into a

goshawk, she flew towards the castle. As she came close the soft glow of lights from the windows helped her identify the correct one. Mentally searching the room, she found someone in there, a man. Swooping past the window, she saw he was in an armchair by a fireplace, his back to her.

Landing on the window ledge, she watched him for a moment before she scanned the room, spotting the desk. It was a large timber desk, dark polished wood with three drawers and brass handles. Another quick look at the man in the armchair showed he was still facing the fire. What was he doing? And what did it matter what he was doing as long as he didn't turn her way.

Heart racing, she dived towards the desk, hiding under the chair, peering out. The man was still in the same place. She pressed against the back of the desk, becoming human. The space was a lot more cramped than she'd thought it would be. Moving the chair a bit, she peered out from beside it. The man hadn't moved. A mental search of the area showed they were still alone. There were people in rooms nearby, but in this one it was only her and the man. Warriors hiding in the Void came to mind, but she dismissed that since no one had stepped out to attack her. Surely anyone who'd seen her wouldn't have let her remain hidden.

Reaching her hand around to the front of the drawers, she grasped the handle, slowly pulling the bottom drawer open. Holding her breath, she flinched when it made a slight sound. The man didn't move. She finished opening the drawer, nearly groaning at the tangle of contents she saw. Didn't dragons believe in throwing crap out? Did they have to keep every single thing that had gone into the drawer for probably the past century?

"Are you in there? What are you doing?" Ronan asked Amber.

She winced, remembering she was meant to have let him know what she saw. *"I'm in, under the desk. There's a man sitting in an armchair facing the fireplace. I've got the bottom drawer open, but it's full of crap, including at least three keys. What if it's not in here?"* She carefully extracted one of the keys, glancing towards the man.

"That's why we have the backup plan of dynamite."

She had to find the key. Setting off the dynamite in that confined an area was a bad idea. Someone was sure to get hurt. Taking another key from the drawer, she placed it on the floor next to the other one. Staring at the man for a moment she waited to see if he'd move. He didn't. Shortly she had all three keys on the floor in front of her and she was eyeing the drawer, wondering if she could manage to dig through the junk without making a sound. It was worse than playing pick-up-sticks when she was younger and she'd never been good at that game.

Carefully pulling out some of the junk, she put it behind her out of the way. Broken pens, a small mirror and a notebook came out next. She shook her head. Why couldn't there just have been the key in the drawer? Maybe with a ribbon tied through it so she could hang it around her neck and fly out of there, without even needing to call Ronan.

The drawer was half empty before she found another key. This was taking too long. Surely there weren't any more keys in the drawer, but she couldn't bring herself to leave before checking.

Right at the bottom was a large, old key, far bigger than the other four keys. *"I'm ready,"* she told Ronan.

"I'll appear by the window."

"Can't you get closer to the desk?"

"No. Be ready to go. I'm coming now."

Scooping up the keys, she ran lightly across the room when Ronan appeared. She wasn't quiet enough. The man spun to face them, rising from his chair as he did so. Amber grabbed hold of Ronan. "Let's go."

"Gair!" Ronan roared.

Amber held onto him when he would have crossed the room. "Let's go."

"He killed my son."

Gair drew his sword. "And I would have eaten his heart if you hadn't got to it first."

"Please. Not now, Ronan. Don't you dare ruin this. He will pay, but not right this moment." She was relieved when Ronan met her gaze, taking them to the crypt through the Void.

"Did you get the key?" Crystal asked.

"What's wrong?" Kade demanded.

Amber shook her head. "Nothing. There was someone in the room." She held up the keys. "I don't know if I've got the right one."

Ronan took the largest key from her and unlocked the door. The moment it swung open, the two guards attacked, distracted by the explosion from outside that could be heard in the lower levels of the castle where they were. No sooner had they dispatched the guards than they faced more as they tried to leave the room. Fighting their way through the depths of the castle, they eventually reached a large room that was empty.

"There's Golds coming in. We're being surrounded in the Void," Crystal said.

"Pull them out," Ronan ordered.

"Kade, look out," Crystal warned.

A Gold momentarily came out of the Void to attack Kade, who barely managed to block before the warrior vanished again.

"Pull them out," Ronan ordered.

"No! They'll pull her in," Flinn said.

"What if someone holds her?" Amber asked.

"I'll hold her. Charles can take them out." Helen held her sword up, her back to her husband as she watched for the enemy. Ronan had given them each a drop of dragon blood to make it easier to communicate with them during the battle.

"Do it," Ronan said.

Helen sheathed her sword, grabbing Crystal around the waist, Charles at her side.

Amber felt uncomfortable with her grandparents wielding weapons, but it was a battle. She couldn't exactly expect them to go into it unarmed. She only hoped they didn't use their swords on any of their temporary allies.

Crystal pulled three people from the Void, Charles taking care of two and Flinn one, before she said, "They've all vanished."

"You know the places you need to check, I have something to deal with." Ronan vanished.

Crystal looked around the room. "He's ditching us?"

"He might know where one of the dragons are that we have to take out." Amber remembered Gair was one of the ones Ronan had mentioned they needed to kill or capture to be able to take his lands back.

"If there are no other dragons to deal with here it's time to keep moving." Charles strode forward, Helen at his side.

Flinn followed. "You're not leading this attack."

Amber nearly groaned. Couldn't they hold off on their arguing at least until the end of the battle? She started to follow when Ronan appeared in front of her and grabbed her arm. She pulled out of his grip. "I'm not going with you."

"He's gone. I need you to find him."

She turned to Rian who had stayed with her, shaking her head when Kade looked behind and started to walk back to her. *"Rian?"*

"Go with him. If you can find one of the ones we are looking for, it will make it easier," Rian said to Amber.

She nodded. *"Explain to Kade."* Turning away from Rian, she reached for Ronan's hand. As soon as his hand tightened around hers, he took them through the Void and back to the library. The room was empty. She searched further away, trying to recall everything she could about the man she'd met for such a short time. "I don't think I can find him. If he's in the Void, you'll need Crystal."

"Wait here." Ronan vanished before Amber could protest.

She swore, looking around nervously. For all she knew she could be surrounded by warriors. They could be standing right next to her and she wouldn't even know. She looked around again, straining to hear the slightest sound, her mind searching the area. What was taking Ronan's so long? Then she realised it was probably Flinn not wanting to part with his mage.

A sound behind her had her spinning, but she didn't get a chance to turn fully when an arm encircled her waist, tightening around her, a knife pressed at her throat.

"What is his plan? He can't take the castle. We've got too many warriors and allies are on the way," Gair said.

Ronan appeared in front of Amber holding Crystal's hand. He let it go and reached for his sword. "If I kill you and your brothers, I've won. The castle will be mine."

"They left to bring back allies. You won't be able to kill them."

"Then I guess I'll just have to make do with you."

Crystal gasped, her hands covering her mouth as she took a step backwards.

Amber felt Gair's arm tighten around her even further. Her gaze met Ronan's and she wondered what he thought he could do.

"Take one step in my direction, or even disappear, and I will kill the girl. Just like I killed your son. You won't be able to save her either."

Amber saw a flicker of something in Ronan's eyes. Pain? Anger? She wasn't certain.

"Amber? What do I do? If I throw ice I might hit you," Crystal said.

"Change. Become a panther. Now!" Ronan ordered.

She pushed away her fear and spoke only to Crystal. *"Nothing. Stay out of the way. Watch for Golds."* Becoming a panther, she twisted in Gair's arms, landing on all fours as Ronan rushed forward, swinging his sword. The smell of blood filled the room and Amber fought the urge to feed, forcing herself to become human again.

"Crystal, check outside the room for Golds," Ronan ordered.

With a nod, Crystal obeyed.

Amber mentally searched the corridor before Crystal left the room, relieved she couldn't find anyone.

Ronan knelt beside Gair, who was still alive. He took a knife and plunged it into his chest, ripping his heart out. As he died, the man turned into a dragon, blood continuing to flow from his wound.

"Flinn wants to know where I am," Crystal told Amber.

Amber searched for Flinn. Finding him, she brought to mind the maps she'd spent ages learning. *"If you fly out the window of the next room and go down a floor and across two windows to your left, you'll find him."*

"Do you need me?"

"No. Go." Amber watched as Ronan rose slowly to his feet, his gaze still on the heart. She didn't know what he planned, but Crystal was better off out of it.

Ronan held the heart out to her.

"What?" She really hoped he didn't expect her to eat it.

"Burn it."

Numerous questions came to mind, but they didn't really have time for her to ask all of them. "Why?"

"Burn it. Now. You won't let me eat it, so burn it. No one else will have the heart of my enemy." He threw the heart on the ground.

She stared at it for a moment, wishing it at least made her feel queasy. When had things like this stopped bothering her? Damn dragons messing with her life. She raised her gaze and met Ronan's. "Tell me what happened when he killed your son."

"He snuck in here ahead of his army. My son was holding the castle for me while I was away. He failed."

That wasn't exactly what she'd wanted to know. "Why'd you eat your son's heart?" Ronan stared at her long enough she was almost certain he wasn't going to answer.

"I arrived to find him ripping my son's heart out. I took it from him. We struggled over it and I turned into a dragon and ate it so he couldn't get it." His gaze was drawn to Gair. "The courtyard filled with warriors and I grabbed my son and left through the Void before they could kill me too." His voice was toneless, his expression hard.

Amber looked away from him, throwing several fireballs at the heart. Her gaze returned to Ronan. "Now what?"

Before Ronan had time to answer, Brann's voice rang in her head. *"Amber! It's Maira. You have to come and save her."*

She had never before heard him sound so panicked. "Take me to Brann." She searched for him and nearly winced. "He's in the courtyard."

"*Amber!*" Brann called her again.

"*I'm coming.*" She grabbed Ronan's arm. "Now. I have to save Maira."

Chapter Twenty-Five

Ronan took her through the Void and they came out amongst heavy fighting, the sun barely risen. Brann had his back to the castle, fighting with a sword. Rian was beside him and Maira lay on the ground behind them, covered in blood. When Amber started to run towards Maira, Ronan pulled her back, taking her through the Void and appearing in a closer location.

Amber knelt beside Maira, pressing her hands against her, trying to heal her friend. "Hang on, Maira." For a moment she couldn't find life, then she did, faint and thready. "Don't you dare go." Amber continued to heal Maira, the sound of battle filling the air behind her. She drew more power from her bracelets, worried at how many she had to drain. "Please, Maira." Her words were a whispered plea as she continued to heal Maira, hoping she didn't become a dragon. The human form was so much easier to heal.

"Their reinforcements are headed this way," Brann warned, then swore. "Ronan's left us."

Maira struggled to sit up. "Amber? What happened?"

Amber crushed Maira to her, not caring about the blood that coated her friend, relief almost overwhelming her. "Stay there. Don't you dare move." She pulled away, rising to her feet, turning towards the battle in time to see Ronan, in dragon form, reappear and drop Gair's body into the middle of the courtyard. Above them, a dragon roared and Ronan streaked higher into the skies.

"They've got reinforcements coming in from the rear," Flinn warned. *"We're outnumbered. We need to retreat."*

"No," Ronan said.

"You're not going to get us killed," Charles warned.

Amber stared at the dragon Ronan fought. The dragon who'd roared when he'd seen Gair's body dumped in the courtyard. *"Jay. Meet me in the courtyard."* She turned into a goshawk and flew upwards.

"I'm coming too," Crystal said.

"You'll stay here," Flinn ordered.

"Not likely," Crystal said.

Amber said to Crystal and Jasper who joined her, *"The dragon Ronan's fighting, take out his wings."*

"Are you sure?" Crystal asked. *"He's not a wyvern. He's a person too."*

She thought of Maira who'd nearly died. There'd been too many close calls. *"They nearly killed Maira. There was a moment when I didn't think I could heal her. We take that dragon out and I believe there's only one more to get rid of and we've won."*

"Our army at the rear of the castle is being slaughtered," Flinn warned.

"Let's do it," Crystal said to Amber and Jasper.

The three of them flew towards Ronan who was still fighting the same dragon. Other dragons tried to join in, but they were engaged by the warriors who'd flown to help Ronan. Amber struck at the wings of the dragon, swooping away when flames came at her. Again she attacked, barely making any difference. It was going to take them forever.

Her heart lurched as she thought of what she needed to do. *"I'm going to burn his wing,"* Amber told Crystal and Jasper.

"Are you crazy?" Crystal demanded.

"What's she planning on doing?" Kade asked.

"Sorry," Crystal said to Amber. *"I forgot not to broadcast. But the question is still the same."*

"I'll take the left wing," Jasper said.

"Done." Amber ignored Crystal's question, flying at the dragon, turning human to cling to his back near his right wing. She hurled a fireball at his wing, managing to throw a second one before she was launched from his back. Falling through the sky, she tried to ignore the pain that hit her as a dragon clawed at her, forcing herself to become a goshawk again. The pain was nearly overwhelming. She struggled to concentrate on her flying.

"You did it," Crystal said. *"He's on the ground and Ronan's tearing him to shreds.*

"The army vanished from the rear of the castle. What's going on?" Flinn demanded.

"Cowards," Ronan said.

Amber landed on the ground, pain making it hard for her to become human again. She stumbled as she turned human, looking at the blood oozing from her side. The wound was worse than she'd thought. Hands held her, lowering her to the ground and she met Ronan's gaze.

"Heal yourself, kitten. Hurry up."

She nodded, trying to follow Ronan's instructions. It was nearly impossible. She frowned when he held up her other hand, then realised he was telling her to draw power from her bracelets.

Arms wrapped around her shoulders. "Amber."

She smiled when Kade spoke her name against her cheek, leaning back against him. She felt so tired.

"Amber!"

Her eyes snapped open and she wondered when she'd shut them. She felt her hand pressed against her side, damp with blood. Then she remembered she was meant to be healing herself. As her wound knitted together, she became more aware of what was going on around her. She was surrounded by worried faces, surprised to see that one of them was her grandmother.

"Did we win?" Her gaze was drawn to Ronan when he chuckled.

"For now, but they'll be back. They'll want revenge," Ronan said.

"That's not our problem," Flinn said.

Ronan held her gaze. "Maybe not."

Amber looked away. She should never have told him that she'd protect him. But what could she have done? He'd known something was wrong. She struggled to stand. "Let me up. I'm fine." She swayed on her feet, glaring at Kade when he put an arm around her waist. "I'm fine," she muttered.

"Come into my castle and sit down," Ronan said.

She was beginning to get used to his predatory smile. That wasn't good. "Why did they run?"

"It would have been because of Laren. He's the weakest of the three brothers. None of his allies would stay and fight if he wasn't going to." Ronan led the way inside.

"So we won," Amber said.

Ronan gave a half shrug. "For now. I'm sure he'll send assassins. That's his style. I'll be ready for them. Eventually I'll get him, but that isn't important right now. I need to install my warriors, deal with the dead and get repairs started."

Amber sat on the wooden bench in the foyer. It was a dark timber, the legs carved in the shape of nightmare-like creatures, their prey dead at their feet. "Whose seat?"

Ronan grinned. "Mine."

Amber rolled her eyes. Typical dragon response. "I meant who put it here."

"It's as old as the castle," Ronan said.

She leaned against Kade as he sat beside her. "That doesn't surprise me. I guess your family have always been a little odd. And bloodthirsty."

Crystal reached out to take Amber's hand. "Are you okay now? You still look pale."

"I'm fine."

"Maybe I shouldn't be having my party tomorrow night. So many people died. So many of our warriors."

"Of course you'll have your party," Ronan said.

"Why?" Crystal asked.

"To celebrate your victory and show your enemies that you're as strong as ever," Ronan said.

"They were only dragons," Charles said.

"Shut up, old man," Flinn growled.

"Time for you to go back in your cage." Ronan grabbed Charles by the arm and they vanished.

When Helen started to complain about high handed dragons, Amber rose to her feet, crossing the space between her and her grandmother. "Did you get hurt?"

"Not a scratch. What were you thinking? I saw what you and your brother did. What would Donna say?"

That's just what she needed, but she wasn't about to let her grandmother hold it over her. She raised her chin. "Tell her, see if I care."

"Amber," Jasper said in warning.

Ronan arrived back and took Helen's arm.

"Wait." Amber grabbed his arm, her gaze on Helen. "I'm glad you're okay. You and Grandad."

"Yes well, it's good you survived too. Donna

would never have stopped crying and I would have had to put up with her carrying on for years."

Amber was surprised at how much the words hurt. She stared at her grandmother a moment longer before she let go of Ronan and he vanished, taking Helen with him.

"She didn't really mean that," Jasper said.

Amber met her brother's gaze. "I think she actually did." She turned away, watching as warriors bustled around them, cleaning up signs of the battle. At least now she knew why her grandmother had never liked them much. "We're not Knights, Jay. In her eyes, that makes us weak and unworthy of her attention." And they never would be Knights. Not true Knights.

Chapter Twenty-Six

"Is it very big?" Donna asked

"Of course it's big. It's a castle." She couldn't believe her mother had asked such a stupid question.

"Will I get to see it one day?"

"How many times do I have to tell you no one can know you're here?" Her mother was driving her crazy. If her uncle didn't hurry up and arrive shortly she'd ditch the entire plan.

Kade drew out his phone and looked at the screen. *"Gary said she's nervous. Let her talk."*

Amber glanced towards Gary who was returning his phone to his pocket. Was he right?

"I know I can't go out there tonight, but later. You'll bring me back here later, won't you?"

Amber eyed her mother. Was she nervous? Maybe. "Sure. Of course I will. And I'll even get Rian to give you the full tour."

"Why can't you give me one?"

"Because I don't know this place like he does." And if her mother asked her as many stupid questions as she had tonight, she'd more than likely lose patience with her and end up in an argument.

"It is your castle, isn't it?" Donna looked at her suspiciously.

"Yes, I'm one of the owners, but so is Rian. He's also my first warrior so it's his job to know this place better than anyone. It's his job to know all my environments."

The door of the planning room opened and Crystal stood in the doorway, a grin on her face. Behind her was Rian and the man from the photo. Roger. Crystal stepped to the side, letting Roger in. Rian remained in the hallway. "The Void is still clear." She closed the door and Roger was left standing with his back against it.

Donna burst into tears. "You look so young."

"Donna?" Roger looked around the room. "I thought I was to meet Amber." His gaze arrowed in on her. "You're Amber?"

She nodded, stepping forward. This wasn't going exactly like she'd planned. "There are no Golds hiding in the Void. No one will know you ever saw your sister. Kade will take her home and everyone will think I wanted our first meeting to be private."

"So she's safe? And my parents? They're all safe?"

"Yeah."

Roger came towards her, wrapping his arms around her, Kade standing away from the wall watching him warily. He turned to Donna, a grin on his face. "I never thought I'd get to see you again." Then he was hugging his sister and both of them were crying and speaking at once.

Amber joined Kade who was leaning against the wall again. "How long do you think we can give them before people start to wonder?"

He shrugged. "Ten minutes?"

"She's not going to be happy to go."

"I'll take Gary back first. Then she can cry on his shoulder instead of mine."

Amber laughed. "Good plan." She looked him up and down. "We don't want to ruin your outfit when you look so good in it." He wore a suit coat and buttoned shirt with his dragon-leather pants.

With a grin, Kade took Gary into the Void, returning a couple of minutes later. He stared at Donna who was still crying and talking quickly, clutching at her brother. "She's your mother. You're the one who has to break the news it's time for her to go."

Amber sighed heavily. She better get it over and done with. "Mum." She stepped closer. "Mum."

"What?" Donna continued to hold onto Roger, staring up at him.

"It's time to go."

"But we've barely spoken."

"Come on, Mum. You promised. We can't risk anyone finding out you were here."

Roger held her from him. "Amber is right. I won't risk you after all these years of protecting you. We'll find another time to meet."

Donna nodded, backing away. "I can't believe how young you look."

"Just say goodbye already," Amber said impatiently.

"Goodbye, Roger." She turned to her daughter. "And you need to be back before the end of the school holidays. I've accepted a dinner invite from Wayne Smith and his daughter for last day of the holidays."

"Mum!"

"No arguments." With a last look at her brother, Donna let Kade take her into the Void. He returned while Roger was still thanking Amber for setting up the meeting.

"Are you both ready to join the celebrations?" Kade looked from one to the other.

Amber nodded. "Yeah. Crystal will be annoyed if we don't put in an appearance at her party. But seriously, how many balls are we going to have to throw in a year?"

Kade slid an arm around her waist. "You'll get used to them."

"I doubt it," Amber muttered. She walked beside Kade, a glance over her shoulder towards her uncle who followed them to the ballroom. There were so many things in her life that needed dealing with.

Her grandparents were demanding to be let go now Ronan's lands had been captured and wouldn't stop telling her about the Knights. Cooper needed somewhere more permanent to stay, Roger had to be released from his promise before her mother risked her life trying to see him and Miles hadn't shown any improvement. There was still another Dragon Mage out there somewhere and an Elder they needed to take down. At least Ronan was happy for the moment, busy taking over his lands. Hopefully that would help slow down his plotting. Although she doubted it.

Crystal pushed through the crowd, tugging Amber away from Kade. "Come and dance with me. I'm seventeen, we own a castle and life is perfect. We have to celebrate."

Amber let Crystal pull her into the dancing crowd, wishing she could feel the same way about everything. She was seventeen and was also an owner of the castle, but life was far from perfect. Crystal threw her head back and laughed, spinning on the spot, arms stretched out, light catching on the diamond necklace they'd recently captured, having begged to borrow it for the ball. Amber grinned. Tomorrow she'd go back to worrying about everything. Tonight Crystal deserved a celebration.

Free Ebook

Subscribe to Avril's newsletter and receive a free ebook. This ebook is exclusive to those on her mailing list. To find out more about this offer visit:

www.avrilsabine.com/free-ebook

*

We value your privacy and will not sell, rent, exchange or loan your email address to third parties. Your information is confidential and you are under no obligation to remain on the mailing list and can unsubscribe at any time.

Acknowledgements

As always, thanks to the usual crew.

To The Reader

If you enjoyed this book, why not consider leaving a review to help other readers discover it too? Reader engagement is one of the few ways that lets an author know readers want more books in a particular series or genre. So leave a review and tell friends, not only about this book but also about other ones you've enjoyed, so you can continue to enjoy books by your favourite authors for years to come.

Dreams are meant to be lived,

Avril.

About The Author

Avril is an Australian author who lives with her family on acreage in South East Queensland. She writes mostly young adult and children's speculative fiction, but has been known to dabble in other genres. You can find more information about her at www.avrilsabine.com where you can also subscribe to her newsletter to be kept informed about new releases, current projects, blog posts and exclusive news.

Titles By Avril Sabine

Stories about strong characters and characters who discover their strengths.

SERIES

Assassins Of The Dead- Young Adult Fantasy/ Paranormal

Book 1: Dark Blade

Book 2: Dragon Touched

Book 3: Society Against Vampires

Book 4: King's Request

Dragon Blood- Young Adult Urban Fantasy (with elements of romance)

(5 book series)

Book 1: Pliethin

Book 2: Wyvern

Book 3: Surety

Book 4: Knight

Book 5: Mage

Dragon Mage- Young Adult Urban Fantasy (with elements of romance)

(Series two of Dragon Blood series)

Book 1: Promise

Dragon Blood Chronicles- Young Adult Urban Fantasy (with elements of romance)

(Companion stand alone series to Dragon Blood)

Book 1: Oath

Book 2: Betrayed

Guardians Of The Round Table- Young Adult Fantasy LitRPG

(Co-written with Storm and Rhys Petersen)

Book 1: Dexterity Fail

Book 2: Goblin Boots

Book 3: Singed Feathers

Book 4: Frog Mage

Book 5: Crystal Mine

Book 6: Cursed Harp

Rosie's Rangers- Young Adult Western Steampunk

(6 book series)

Book 1: Justice

Book 2: Vengeance

Book 3: Treachery

Book 4: Accused

Book 5: Wanted

Book 6: Corruption

Mark Of Kings- Children's Fantasy

(Upper middle grade/preteen)

(4 book series)

Book 1: The Arena

Book 2: The Island

Book 3: The Assassin

Book 4: The King

STAND ALONE SERIES

Demon Hunters- Young Adult Urban Fantasy/ Horror (with elements of romance)

Book 1: Blood Sacrifice

Book 2: Retribution

Book 3: Tainted

Book 4: Premonition

Book 5: Cursed

Book 6: Feud

Book 7: Extrication

Plea Of The Damned- *Young Adult Urban Fantasy/Paranormal*

(6 book series)

Book 1: Forgive Me Lucy

Book 2: Forgive Me Aiden

Book 3: Forgive Me Jena

Book 4: Forgive Me Kobe

Book 5: Forgive Me Marti

Book 6: Forgive Me Dawson

Realms Of The Fae- *Young Adult Urban Fantasy* (*with elements of romance*)

The Sword (short story in Like A Girl Anthology)

Heart Of Stone

Book 1: A Debt Owed

Book 2: Marked By The Hunt

Book 3: The Magic Collector

Book 4: An Unexpected Betrayal

Book 5: Imprisoned By Iron

Fairytales Retold (Short Stories)

Snow-White And Rose-Red

The Twelve Brothers

The Light Princess

Beauty And The Beast

Sleeping Beauty

Aschenputtel

The Golden Bird

The Frog Prince

The Death Of Koshchei The Deathless

Myths And Legends Retold (Short Stories)

Ion, Son Of Apollo

Sir Gawain And The Maid With The Narrow Sleeves

Princess Ilse, The Giant's Daughter

YOUNG ADULT NOVELS

Young Adult Fantasy (with elements of romance)

Elf Sight

Earth Bound

Young Adult Urban Fantasy

Stone Warrior (with elements of romance)

The Jungle Inside

Young Adult Contemporary (with elements of romance)

Through Your Eyes

The Ugly Stepsister

Perfect Little Princess

Young Adult Contemporary/Paranormal

Whispers In The Dark (with elements of romance and same sex relationships)

Over Too Soon (with elements of romance)

Young Adult Sci-Fi

Experiment X-One-Six (Urban Sci-Fi/Superheroes)

An Endless Dawn (Post Apocalyptic Sci-Fi)

CHILDREN'S BOOKS

Dragon Lord (Preteen/early teens) (Fantasy)

The Irish Wizard (Upper middle grade) (Urban Fantasy)

SHORT STORIES

Urban Fantasy

Eternally Late

Dealings With Joe

Glimpses (short story in That Moment When Anthology)

Contemporary

The Brat Next Door

Fantasy LitRPG

(Set in the same world as Guardians Of The Round Table Series)

Tales Of Inadon 1: The Disc (Co-written with Storm and Rhys Petersen) (short story in Game On! Anthology)

Post Apocalyptic Sci-Fi

Compulsive Directive

NONFICTION

A Year Of Weekly Writing Exercises (Creative Writing)

Cooking For Families With Allergies (Cooking) (Co-written with Storm Petersen)

Tell Me A Story, Grandma (Memoir)

For the most up to date details on available titles visit:

www.avrilsabine.com/books/bibliography

Dragon Blood Series

To learn more about this series visit:

www.avrilsabine.com/series/db

BOOKS AVAILABLE IN THE DRAGON BLOOD SERIES

(5 book series)

Book 1: Pliethin

Book 2: Wyvern

Book 3: Surety

Book 4: Knight

Book 5: Mage

BOOKS SET IN THE SAME WORLD AS THE DRAGON BLOOD SERIES

Dragon Mage- Young Adult Urban Fantasy (with elements of romance)

(Series two of Dragon Blood series)

Book 1: Promise

Dragon Blood Chronicles- Young Adult Urban Fantasy (with elements of romance)

(Companion stand alone series to Dragon Blood)

Book 1: Oath

Book 2: Betrayed

Disclaimer

This is a work of fiction. Names, characters, businesses, places, events and incidents are either the products of the author's imagination or used in a fictitious manner. Any resemblance to actual persons, living or dead, or actual events is purely coincidental. The opinions expressed or beliefs held are those of the characters and should not be assumed to be the opinions or beliefs of the author.